"When you look at me like that," Malik said as he brought his mouth toward hers, **"you make it hard for me to deny myself a taste."**

"Then don't," she said, causing him to halt right before his lips touched hers.

He searched her eyes, and instead of kissing her, he moved to her neck, placing a soft kiss right behind her ear. His tongue swirled small circles on her sweet spot until Mya released a soft moan. The teasing was over as quickly as it started.

Malik snaked one arm behind her back and pulled her into his embrace as his other hand went behind her head. Slowly, he brought his lips down on hers in such a seductive way that Mya had barely processed what they were doing until they were already doing it.

She felt his kiss all the way in her toes, feeding her desire even more. Just as she'd predicted, lips like his were made for kissing, and the gentle, methodical movement of his tongue reached parts of her that no man had ever even come close to reaching before.

Forgotten was the fact that she had been holding up her dress. But instead of caring that the material was now lying on the floor, she was more concerned with her wish for his towel to join her dre

D0187855

Dear Reader,

Meet Mya Winters. And Malik Madden, the hero determined to break the barriers around Mya's heart. I knew from the minute I wrote about Malik's character in *A Tempting Proposal* that he was the perfect hero for the feisty yet fabulous Mya.

Writing the love story for the final Elite Events founder was exciting, yet sad at the same time. But I'm currently working on a new series featuring cousins of a few characters you've met before! I just couldn't resist giving the Elite Event founders an opportunity to make a guest appearance in my new series.

I hope you enjoy Mya and Malik's journey as much as I enjoyed writing it. I love hearing from readers, so please feel free to contact me.

Much love,

Sherelle

AuthorSherelleGreen@gmail.com

@sherellegreen

Beautiful
Surrender

Sherelle Green

HARLEQUIN® KIMANI™ ROMANCE

If you purchased this book without a cover you should be aware
that this book is stolen property. It was reported as "unsold and
destroyed" to the publisher, and neither the author nor the
publisher has received any payment for this "stripped book."

Recycling programs
for this product may
not exist in your area.

ISBN-13: 978-0-373-86403-4

Beautiful Surrender

Copyright © 2015 by Sherelle Green

All rights reserved. The reproduction, transmission or utilization of this
work in whole or in part in any form by any electronic, mechanical or
other means, now known or hereinafter invented, including xerography,
photocopying and recording, or in any information storage or retrieval
system, is forbidden without written permission. For permission please
contact Harlequin Kimani, 225 Duncan Mill Road, Toronto, Ontario
M3B 3K9, Canada.

This is a work of fiction. Names, characters, places and incidents are
either the product of the author's imagination or are used fictitiously,
and any resemblance to actual persons, living or dead, business establishments,
events or locales is entirely coincidental.

® and TM are trademarks of Harlequin Enterprises Limited or its corporate
affiliates. Trademarks indicated with ® are registered in the United States
Patent and Trademark Office, the Canadian Intellectual Property Office and in
other countries.

For questions and comments about the quality of this book please contact us
at CustomerService@Harlequin.com.

HARLEQUIN®
™ www.Harlequin.com

Printed in U.S.A.

Sherelle Green is a Chicago native with a dynamic imagination and a passion for reading and writing. Her love for romance developed in high school after stumbling across a hot-and-steamy Harlequin novel. She instantly became an avid romance reader and decided to pursue an education in English and journalism. A true romantic, she believes in predestined romances, love at first sight and fairy-tale endings.

Books by Sherelle Green

Harlequin Kimani Romance

A Tempting Proposal
If Only for Tonight
Red Velvet Kisses
Beautiful Surrender

Visit the Author Profile page at Harlequin.com for more titles.

To my grandparents, John, Gladys, Hazel and James. Each of you has played an extremely important role in my life, and I feel so blessed to have you as grandparents. Papa John, I received my determination and fortitude from you… Always hardworking, never yielding and always striving to succeed, provide and educate. Grandma Gladys, I received my compassion, spirit and love for life from you… Always living life to its fullest, warm soul to the core and loving your family and close friends with every piece of your heart. Grandma Hazel, I received my inner strength and ability to compose great stories from you… Always sharing a piece of yourself and your heart to better someone else while your stories and reflections make memories for generations. Papa James, I received my sense of humor and quick thinking from you… Always striving to place a smile on someone's face and always thinking fast on your feet, teaching us that the key to a happy life is to always wear a smile. Each of you has overcome so much adversity, and because of the values and beliefs you instilled in your children and grandchildren, we are confident. We are compassionate. But more important, we are loved!

Acknowledgments

To my bestie Alexandria "Alex"—when we first met, I knew you would be the friend of a lifetime. You aren't afraid to take chances and truly live life to the fullest. The ultimate go-getter, you always strive to succeed. Your quick-fire wittiness never ceases to amaze me, and I love the fact that you remain true to your character no matter what the circumstance. Years ago, we made a promise to always support each other's goals and dreams. At the time, we had no idea what path life would take us down. Your journey has inspired me in so many ways. We've had so many great and amazing times together and I am so proud of you. Thank you so much for your friendship…LYLAS!

Prologue

"Say one more word to me and you'll be walking around this wedding reception decorated with this delicious glass of expensive white wine." As Mya Winters gracefully walked away from the current subject of her irritation, she hoped the intensity in her eyes had provided extra warning.

Her four-inch turquoise heels clicked against the smooth cranberry-wood surface of the massive deck adorned in a variety of exotic floral arrangements. Before she could reach the other side that overlooked the Caribbean Sea, a strong hand grabbed her arm.

She turned abruptly, her eyes traveling from the hand on her arm to the face of a man who clearly didn't understand the meaning of leaving her alone.

When the annoying pick-up lines that he'd been using on her all night continued to spurt from his mouth, she couldn't help the jolt of her hand as the remnants in her glass of wine made contact with his face.

"I can't believe you just did that you b—"

"Keep talking and one of my heels will get friendly with a part of your body that I'm sure you'll need in the future," Mya said, cutting off whatever he had been about to say. She crossed her arms over her chest before she continued. "Although it doesn't really matter since it's evident that the lack of style in your walk is directly proportionate to the way you handle business in the bedroom…quick and sloppy."

The man frantically looked around the crowded wedding reception to see who had overheard Mya's comment. Noticing that they had garnered more than enough attention, he placed his hands on his drenched face and muttered expletives as he finally walked away from her.

"Did you really have to throw your wine at him?" asked Lex Turner, Mya's business partner and friend, as she approached.

"Well, he wouldn't shut up," Mya said as quietly as she could. "Besides, I gave him several warnings to leave me the hell alone."

"Mya," Lex said leading her farther away from the crowd. "This is Cyd and Shawn's dream wedding. It isn't like you to show out at important events. What's going on?"

Mya casted her eyes to the floor, refusing to look Lex in the eye in fear she would see through the lie she was about to tell. "Nothing's wrong. I guess I'm just a little tired from all the events I had to plan before the wedding."

Mya Winters and her partners Lexus Turner, Imani Rayne-Barker and Cydney Rayne—who was now officially Cydney Rayne-Miles—were the owners of Elite Events Incorporated in Chicago, Illinois. What had once started as a dream was now an established event-planning company, and business was thriving in ways the foursome had never imagined.

"I don't believe you," Lex stated. "But I'm sure you'll tell me when you're ready. In the meantime, can you try to refrain from dousing wine on every man that approaches you tonight?"

"I will make no such promise."

"Mya!" Lex exclaimed.

"Okay, okay," Mya replied as she waved her hands in the air. "For the rest of the night, my wine will stay in my glass." *Unless another sorry excuse for a man decides that tonight is the night he wants to challenge me.*

Lex shot her another look of disbelief before she walked off to join her fiancé, Micah Madden. Mya watched Lex softly kiss her soon-to-be-husband, before witnessing a similar exchange between Imani and her husband, Daman, and newlyweds, Cyd and Shawn.

"All this cuteness is making me nauseous," she said to herself before grabbing a glass of wine from a nearby waiter and taking a large gulp of the smooth liquid.

"Try not to throw this one," the male waiter said with a laugh as he walked away.

"That was cute," Mya said with slight disregard. She shot the waiter a strained smile before setting her wistful gaze back on her friends. It wasn't that she was jealous of her friends' relationships. She was actually really happy for them and glad they had each found the man of their dreams.

But she couldn't help but be a bit jealous of the happiness reflected in their eyes. A happiness she hadn't felt in a really long time.

Ever since I got that phone call, she thought. There weren't many things in life that surprised Mya, but getting a discreet phone call from someone who seemed to know something about her past was definitely unexpected and she had been in a foul mood for the past week because of it.

Growing up in foster care and witnessing things that no child ever deserved to see, had dismissed any fantasies she had about having a life that resembled one plucked from a classic fairy tale. Real life wasn't filled with happily-ever-afters and knights in shiny armor. Maybe for some it was, but never for her. Despite Mya's love for her foster mother, Ms. Bee, who'd been her savior after a slew of terrible foster homes, there wasn't any part of her childhood that could be remotely viewed as perfect.

Taking another sip of her wine, Mya sighed deeply. Now wasn't the time for a pity party. Just as she was about to continue her journey to the somewhat empty side of the deck, a loan figure caused her to avert her eyes in another direction. He stopped to talk to a few other people as he made his way back to the group, but it was his walk that had caught her attention. *Confident. Powerful. Purposeful.* She knew him, of course. This wasn't the first time she'd noticed his walk and with all the love in the air, her hormones were surely acting wacky.

She tried to will herself to look away from Mr. Tall, Dark and Handsome. But as usual, she never seemed to tear her gaze away fast enough. She let her eyes roam over his athletic build that was encased in light gray beachwear attire identical to the other groomsmen. By the time her gaze made it to his face, she wasn't surprised to find his eyes locked on hers.

Why on earth did he always have to look so sexy? Since the first day she'd met private investigator Malik Madden, the Ivy League graduate had been getting under her skin in the best way possible. Today he was sporting a pair of stylish black glasses that made him look even sexier than usual. Mya wasn't usually even attracted to men who wore glasses, but she found that she missed them whenever Malik chose not to wear them.

As if it weren't bad enough, they had been paired together for the current wedding and were paired again later this year for another wedding. They also both held major parts in each. It had become difficult for their friends not to pair them together during rehearsals and prewedding events.

The slight breeze that caught her hair was a friendly reminder that she should continue her journey to the other side of the deck and stop playing eye tag with Malik. Giving him one more thorough glance, she downed the rest of her wine before walking off.

"Damn, bro," Micah said, slapping Malik's shoulder. "If you ever decide to actually tell Mya how much you're interested in her, maybe you should skip talking to her in front of large groups of people or any other public displays of affection."

Malik shook his head at his younger brother, never taking his eyes off Mya's legs. "I'll keep that in mind," he said raising an eyebrow at Micah. "She's really not all that bad."

Micah almost spit his drink out across the floor. "Dude, did you just see her berate Shawn's friend who tried to talk to her?"

"Yeah, I saw it," Malik said with a shrug as he took a swig of his Corona.

"She basically castrated him with those words," Micah exclaimed. "No female at this wedding will go two feet near him now."

"He's always been a jerk anyway," Malik replied, finally willing his gaze to move beyond her legs. When he did, he was satisfied to find her checking him out just as thoroughly. She always looked great every time he saw her, but tonight, seeing her in a short turquoise strapless dress was pushing his desire to another limit.

"Jerk or not, Mya's tongue is lethal and ever since I got with Lex, I've watched her dismiss plenty of guys who have tried to get close to her but failed."

Malik turned slightly to the side to regard his brother. "Are you saying you don't think I could handle a woman like Mya?"

"That's exactly what I'm saying, bro," Micah said with a laugh. "Mya's really cool to hang out with and she's beautiful. I even like that she can watch sports with Shawn and I just like one of the guys. But to date her? I think you'd have your hands full."

Malik shook off his brother's warning, knowing it was already too late for him. He'd made up his mind years ago, the first time he saw her at Daman and

Imani's wedding, that he would make her his one day. He'd attended that wedding with his ex, Alicia, and even then, he hadn't been able to take his eyes off Mya.

"Besides," Micah said. "Mya is feisty as hell. And no offense, bro, but you never did do well with spontaneous women like her since you're…um…you just overthink things too much."

Malik looked away from Micah. He already knew what he was about to say. While Micah had been playing with the neighborhood kids back when they lived in Little Rock, Arkansas, Malik had been inside studying for advanced placement classes. Although they were close, Malik and Micah were like night and day. But Malik didn't like being labeled as the *boring* brother who always followed the rules. Following the rules had certainly helped with his career, but hadn't worked so well when it came to women and relationships.

"Oh ye of little faith," Malik said gripping Micah's shoulder and brushing off his words. "When will you learn not to underestimate your big brother?"

Micah shook his head in disbelief. "Don't say I didn't warn you." Malik barely heard Micah's words as he continued to observe Mya's blatant appraisal of him. He didn't understand why their chemistry was so intense, but as it usually went with them, he locked his eyes to her face and waited for her to make direct contact. When she cast her coffee-colored eyes on his deep mahogany ones, he felt the intensity of their connection throughout his entire body.

He could have stood there and stared at her all night, but she broke the moment, gave him a slight smile, and walked away. Only when she left did Malik let his breath rush from his lips, and then he took a final swig of his beer.

"But on the other hand," Micah said. "I never see her look at anyone the way she looks at you. So maybe she's just waiting for you to make a move."

Malik didn't know if Micah had told him that in hopes that he'd make a fool of himself and prove him right, or if he actually believed what he was saying. Regardless, it didn't matter because there was no doubt in his mind that he could handle all that Mya was willing to offer and more. Making up his mind, he passed Micah his empty beer bottle and followed after Mya.

The Anguilla beach on a hot March night was truly a beautiful sight. But even the warm wind looping through Mya's brown curls and the festive reggae music couldn't ease her mind. Taking off her heels, she stepped off the deck. She then placed her pedicured toes in the white sand and began walking toward the ocean.

Even in the nighttime, she could see shadows of couples on the beach wrapped up in their own love cocoon. As she stood there, gazing out at the ocean, she welcomed the darkness that hid the sadness written across her face. *I'll just stand like this for a few minutes and then I'll rejoin the party and put on my best smile*, she thought to herself as she closed her eyes. She was determined not to waste any more time on her friend's special day thinking about the call she wished she hadn't received. Besides, she was leaving for the airport the next morning to meet with some members of the Chicago community about the current status of two after-school programs that were in danger of closing. She had to make sure that her brain was clear for her meeting.

"I love the sound of the ocean at night," she whispered. Her eyes remained closed, but she was well aware that someone else had joined her on the beach and was standing close by. The light scent of Giorgio Armani cologne proved that it was the one person she wished hadn't followed her to the beach. Not because she was prepared to subject him to the same verbal warning that she had given to the guy who had hit on her earlier, but because she knew he was the one man who made her feel so unlike herself.

"It really is a beautiful sound."

Mya slowly lifted her head and peered over to the man who owned the deep, penetrating voice that caused shivers to run throughout her body.

"Are you enjoying the wedding?" Malik asked, staring back at her.

"Of course," she said with a smile. "It's everything that Cyd and Shawn wanted."

"Think you'll ever get married one day?" The question he asked would've been simple if it had come from any other man, but coming from Malik, it made her pause before responding.

"Probably not," she finally replied. "What about you?"

"Not in the cards for me, either, although my mom is trying to convince me to go out with her friend's daughter. Micah getting engaged before me is really complicating my life," he said with a laugh.

"That's understandable," Mya said, joining in his

laughter as she remembered the way Cynthia Madden had inquired about her love life when she realized Mya was still single on the day Micah proposed to Lex.

They stood in comfortable silence for a few minutes before Malik began to speak again. "Listen," he said stepping a little closer to her. "I have some business to take care of in Chicago next week so after I leave here I won't be going right back to Detroit."

"I'm leaving tomorrow," Mya replied as she tried to stall the question she knew Malik would ask and averted her eyes back to the ocean.

"So I was wondering," Malik continued, staring directly at her and ignoring her attempt to sidetrack him. Even in the darkness, she could feel the intensity in his eyes. "Would you like to go out with me sometime next week?"

Ugh! Why did he have to ask me out? "Listen," Mya said as she tried to think about the best way to decline and not come off as rude. "I appreciate the offer, but I have to pass. I can't go out with you."

"Okay," he said, turning back to the ocean. "May I ask why?"

I wish you wouldn't. "I just have a lot going on and I don't have time to date."

She could feel the tension in the air and knew he still had more questions.

"I understand," he said, rubbing his hand across the back of his neck. "But one date couldn't hurt."

I really don't have time for this. Mya actually did like Malik, but she didn't want to date him or any other man right now. She had way too much going on in her personal life and dating Malik, a man who knew all her friends, meant that he was too close to her life. If things didn't work out, where would that leave them? Mya knew the deal. One date would turn into two dates, and then three dates. Next thing they knew, everyone would be celebrating their wedding and proclaiming what a cute couple they were. It had happened to Imani, Cyd and recently engaged Lex.

She laughed aloud at the direction of her thoughts. The man had asked her on one date and she was already predicting how badly it could end. Nonetheless, she knew her decision was a solid *no*.

"How about we just stick to seeing each other at friendly gatherings," Mya finally replied.

Malik gave her a sly smile. "For now," he added before he began walking back to the deck. Mya turned around to watch him walk away until he faded into the darkness.

Malik was sweet, nice and definitely not equipped to understand her complicated life. *He would never be able to handle me*, she thought, turning back to the ocean.

Chapter 1

Two months later...

There was nothing cuter than an adorable little guy with smooth creamy brown skin, piercing round honey eyes and a head full of curly brown hair.

"It's official, I think I'm in love," Mya Winters said softly as she placed a hand over her heart and gazed down at the face of her newest addiction.

"He's such a ladies' man," said Mya's friend and Elite Events cofounder, Imani Rayne-Barker. "I think he has a crush on you."

"I think he does too," Mya replied as her heart swelled with pride. "Hey, little guy," she cooed while touching the hands of the smallest human she'd ever held. "It's Auntie Mya and I've been thinking about another promise I want to make to you. I promise to always give you cookies and teach you all the things your mom doesn't want me to teach you."

"Really, Mya," Imani said, her voice filled with laughter. Imani and her husband, Daman Barker, were the proud parents of Daman Stanley Barker Jr., who everyone affectionately called DJ.

"You are the cutest thing I've ever seen," she exclaimed as she rocked DJ in her arms. He laughed in a way that proved he agreed with her statement. He caught ahold of her pinkie finger and gently tugged, rewarded by a large smile from Mya.

"He's only five weeks old and you already spoil him way too much," Imani said as she walked around her living room picking up an array of shopping bags filled with clothes and toys for DJ that Mya had lugged through the door earlier.

"I can't help it," Mya said as she made funny faces at DJ. "He deserves the best."

Imani opened her mouth to speak, but was interrupted by her husband, Daman.

"The rest of the clan is here," Daman announced as he walked into the room followed by Cyd and Lex.

Imani stood to hug them, but the two women went straight to Mya who was still making funny faces at DJ.

"I'm next," Cyd said taking DJ out of Mya's arms after promising Mya that she would give him back soon. "How's my handsome nephew doing?" She brushed noses with DJ who raised his little hands to cup her face.

"I love it when he does that," Lex said observing the exchange between Cyd and DJ before she placed more shopping bags in the corner of the living room where Imani had neatly stacked the bags from Mya.

"No love for me?" Imani said reaching out her arms. Lex walked over and gave her a quick hug.

"Sorry, sis," Cyd said, making no attempt to move. "I've been waiting all day to hold DJ."

"I can't wait until you guys have kids so that y'all can see how it feels to be ignored." Mya laughed at her friend's comment. Imani was the most motherly of the group so Mya knew she loved the attention DJ was getting. Happiness was reflected in her eyes every time she looked at DJ.

Mya wasn't the mushy or sentimental type, but being around DJ brought out feelings in her that she hadn't ever felt before. Not having a family of her own meant she missed normal family milestones like graduations, birthday parties, first births of the family and the overall feeling of belonging.

"How about I take my son with me to the next room while you ladies get started on business," Daman announced to the room. He reached his arms out to a reluctant Lex who had just tugged DJ from Cyd. After giving the infant a small peck, Lex handed DJ over to his father.

"Okay, since I called this meeting, I'll start," Mya said as she slipped a few sheets of paper out of her bag. Ever since Imani had given birth to DJ, there had been more meetings hosted at Imani and Daman's estate with a gorgeous view of Lake Michigan, than the Elite Events office in downtown Chicago. Choosing Imani's home to host their weekly Monday meetings gave Mya, Cyd and Lex a chance to see DJ who had quickly become the main reason any of them went shopping anymore.

"As I discussed a few months ago, there is a huge problem with the two after-school programs that we sponsor in conjunction with Chicago Public Schools." Mya handed each of the women a sheet of paper. "A few days ago, the advisory board informed me that the programs would be shutting down in a couple months. Our efforts to save the programs didn't help."

"How is that possible?" Imani asked as she scanned over the notes on the paper. "We received more investments over the past couple months for this school year than ever before."

"I know," Mya said in irritation as she thought about her meeting with the board. "Apparently, since so many CPS schools closed last year and even more the year before, enrollment in the after-school programs was extremely low. The money we received from investors wasn't enough to cover all the costs."

"Sounds like BS to me," Cyd stated as she crossed her arms over her chest. "Enrollment is never that expensive, so the money they would have gotten would have been minimal anyway. Seems suspicious."

"Don't even get me started," Mya said as she waved her hands in the air. "I've already raised hell, but it's not doing any good. There are plenty of CPS teachers and employees still upset about the direction of our schools and after-school programs. Most of our voices are going unheard. It's getting better, but there's still a long journey ahead."

Overseeing programs Elite Events sponsored was always something that Mya enjoyed. Especially managing the after-school programs. If Mya hadn't started

Elite Events Inc. with her partners, she would have definitely been a public school teacher. Through the after-school programs, she still put her love for education to good use despite the obstacles she was currently faced with.

"I remember a time when the Monday news didn't consist of a summary of shootings that happened over the weekend. But this is still a great city and you all know how much I value education. It seems that there are fewer opportunities to keep students in school and out of the streets. The youth needs these programs now more than ever."

Mya had devoted a lot of time and energy into the programs, and Elite Events had invested large amounts of money to keep them from shutting down. "It's time for us to take matters into our own hands."

"Are you thinking about a plan to try and save the after-school programs?" Lex asked.

"Even better," Mya replied as she reached in her bag once more and pulled out three portfolios. "Instead of investing more money and allowing the board to control these programs, I think we should open our own after-school program."

She handed each woman a portfolio containing all the details about the Chicagoland location where they would headquarter the program, and a list of teachers and employees who currently worked at the other two after-school programs who had expressed interest in working for the Elite Events After-School Program if they chose to take that route.

"This all seems great," Imani said scrolling through the pages. "And I agree that there are plenty of students who could benefit from us funding our own program. But even though business is booming, how can we afford this initiative?"

"I was hoping you would ask," Mya said with a smile. "I didn't include these details in the portfolio, but I've been losing sleep over how we can get the initial money needed to fund this program despite the fact that we'd be utilizing the building and staff of one of the closing locations."

Mya scooted to the edge of her seat, excited to share her plan with the ladies. "We meet so many influential people in our line of work and so many of them are single. What do you guys think about Elite Events hosting the first annual Elite Events Charity Date Auction? If all goes well, we could host one every year."

"Oh, I like that," Lex replied while Cyd and Imani expressed similar sentiments.

"This charity date auction will be unlike any other auction that Chicagoans have seen before. Tickets for the auction will cost a small fee and the highest bidder gets to go on a date with his or her bid. All proceeds will go to the 'save our after-school programs' fund, only in true Elite Events fashion, we will host a dream date for the six winning couples from the audience chosen by a random draw. Therefore, singles get a chance to bid on their favorite participant and possibly win one of six dates after all the participants have been auctioned off. I know next month is soon, but we need to raise the money before school starts after Labor Day. What does everyone think?"

Mya sat back in her seat and waited anxiously for their opinions.

"I think it's a great idea," Lex replied with a smile.

"Maybe we should hold an informational meeting for the participants too."

"I love it too," Cyd added. "When we have a solid plan, I'll reach out to a few of our friends in the media."

Imani looked up from the portfolio she was still scanning. "I really think you're on to something, Mya," she said excitedly. "This charity date auction will get Chicagoans who aren't usually concerned with education excited about contributing to a greater cause. There's only one thing really missing from this plan."

Mya studied Imani's expression. "Which would be what exactly?"

Imani glanced from Cyd to Lex before setting her eyes back on Mya. "A sexy male cohost, of course."

"Cohost a date auction? For what?" Malik asked as he propped up his iPhone on his grand dark cherry desk and shuffled through a cluster of file folders.

"You really need to quit being so old school sometimes," Micah said as his eyes scanned over Malik's desk. Malik ignored the jab, but he had to agree with Micah. The colorful array of folders was another reminder that he really needed to digitally document his old files before the end of the year.

"I am digital with most of my client files. I need to be since I'm always traveling. These are old files from over six years ago that I haven't had time to document online." He was trying his best to concentrate on what Micah was explaining to him, but as usual, Micah seemed to be up to something.

"You FaceTimed me right before an important

meeting to ask me to do something you know I won't do and to criticize the way I organize my office?" Malik wasn't agreeing to cohost anything until he knew exactly why Micah thought he'd be interested. When his brother began spurting random analogies that compared Malik to his fiancée, Lex, who was also a cautious thinker, he didn't have the patience to wait any longer for the catch.

"Spit it out, Micah," he said as he leaned back in his oversized desk chair and slightly turned to view beads of rain cascade down the side of his Detroit office window.

"Elite Events is hosting their first charity date auction next month and they are looking for a cohost for the event."

"Next month? That's really soon."

"They know," Micah replied. "They need to move quickly because the funds from the date auction will help them fund a new after-school program that will accept all of the students from two programs that are closing. They need everything finalized before Labor Day."

"I'd be happy to donate," Malik said as he twirled his chair to a small black filing cabinet and placed some folders back in their appropriate place. "But I'm not really into cohosting events like this. I'm sure the ladies would rather someone else cohost whose presence will bring in extra money and someone who permanently resides in Chicago."

"Naw, bro. For whatever reason, they think you would be great as a cohost. I told Lex that you wouldn't be interested, but she thinks there is at least one reason you won't be able to turn them down."

Malik already had a feeling that he knew what that reason was, but he wanted to hear Micah confirm his suspicions. "And what might that be?"

"Mya is the lead on planning this project and is also hosting the charity date auction."

"I figured," Malik said with a laugh as he turned back to his phone and clasped his large hands together. "Does Mya know about the ladies asking me to cohost?"

"I doubt it," Micah answered. "Which is why I knew this call was pointless and you wouldn't do it. I noticed that you and Mya didn't really talk much at Shawn and Cyd's wedding after you went after her. I warned you she was tough to handle."

Malik could admit that things with Mya hadn't exactly gone as planned, but he wasn't giving up on his pursuit of her. She may have said one thing, but her body language that night had contradicted her words.

The charity date auction would give him a chance to be around her more. Since they didn't live in the same state, he didn't see her much and that definitely needed to change if he was going to pursue her.

"Tell you what," Malik said leaning back in his desk chair. "I'll cohost the event under one condition." Micah asked Malik to explain. "Tell the ladies that I want to be the one to tell Mya that I'm cohosting the charity date auction."

"Um, I don't think that's a good idea."

Malik raised an eyebrow at Micah. "Like you didn't pull the same thing when you convinced the ladies to make Lex plan our parents' anniversary party."

"That was different," Micah interjected. "Only Lex

and Mya were free to plan the party anyway. But hold on while I tell her what you said."

Malik waited patiently as he stared at his phone and observed the photos on Micah's wall. The framed pictures were from a couple different family events. There was one photo of his parents and another candid photo of Micah and Lex when Micah had proposed. But the photo that caught his attention was the one that had been taken of the entire group at their engagement party. It was another candid shot and most people were laughing or cheering in the photo. He spotted himself in the back of the group on one side of the picture with Mya a few people down from where he stood.

Malik remembered the exact moment the shot was taken. He had been staring at Mya for most of the day, intrigued by the mystery behind her gaze. He had wondered what she had been thinking and had decided to approach her just as he heard the round of applause and tore his gaze away from her to cheer for his brother and Lex when they walked into the room.

Malik leaned in closer to his screen, wishing Face-Time had a zoom-in option so he could see the photo better. When he concluded that he couldn't, he paused his FaceTime and searched through his emails to see if Lex had included that particular photo in the hundreds she'd sent him from the party. Luckily, she had grouped the photos and he was able to find the one he had been searching for. When he did, he zoomed in on his face in the photo before sliding his finger across the screen to view Mya.

"How did I miss that?" he said to himself as he noticed Mya's face in the photo for the first time. Her face may have been turned towards Micah and Lex, but her eyes were definitely pointed in his direction. There was no guarantee that she was looking at him, but his gut was telling him that she was.

"Malik, you still there?"

Malik exited his email and returned to his Face-Time chat with his brother. "Yeah, I'm still here, what did she say?"

"You are one lucky man, my dude. Lex said that she could set up a meeting with Mya so that you can be the one to tell her the news. She'll contact you to discuss the details."

"Sounds good," Malik responded. After briefly catching up about work and family, Malik disconnected the call. He peered out the window at the light gray sky and wondered how Mya would take the news. He knew she wouldn't like it, but maybe Mya was too professional to let him know how she really felt about him being the cohost.

Chapter 2

"You have got to be kidding me," Mya said loudly with both hands on her hips as she paced back and forth. "No offense, but you don't exactly strike me as the type to host an event like this. I'm pretty sure hosting a retirement party is more your speed."

Hosting a retirement party? He turned an eyebrow up at her as he listened to Mya's voice bounce across the office walls. He had been in her office for ten minutes and Mya still seemed as irritated by the idea as she had when he had first delivered the news.

Malik would be the first to admit that he didn't exactly go club hopping every weekend. But in all his almost thirty-four years he had never had a woman make assumptions about him like the ones that were spurting from Mya's mouth. A mouth that he wasn't sure needed taming with words or his lips. Since he

was pretty sure she would slap him across the face
if he dared to pull her into his arms and silence her
with a breathtaking kiss, he figured words were his
only ally.

"Hear me out," he said, getting up from the sturdy
chair. "I was surprised that the women wanted me to
cohost too. But like it or not, we are in this together
and I never break a commitment. Besides," he continued as he stepped a little closer to her. "I happen
to know a lot of professional singles in the Detroit
area, as well as other Midwest cities, so we can use
my connections to our advantage by pulling in as
many influential people as possible." Although he
had been hesitant to accept at first, now that he was
committed to hosting the event, he planned on doing
a damn good job at it.

"Right. Because that makes all the difference,"
Mya mumbled sarcastically as she finally stopped
pacing. "Look, I know that you're well connected. But
this charity date auction is really important to me. You
have to be personable and engaging. Yes, it's great
that you have connections, but...never mind." Mya
crossed her arms over her chest in slight irritation.

Malik gave her a stern look as he contemplated
what he should say next. A part of him wanted to tell
her to finish her statement. But he knew she'd only
stopped herself because the words that had been on
the tip of her tongue were unpleasant.

"Mya, I understand that this may not be the most
ideal situation for you."

"You think?" she said cutting him off.

"But like it or not, I'm your cohost," he continued,
ignoring her interjection.

Her arms remained crossed, but her facial expression softened.

"This is a huge commitment because the event is next month. You don't even live in Chicago, so I assume you're fine with traveling back and forth from Detroit in case you're needed before the event. I have to be able to rely on you."

Malik studied Mya's expression and shook his head in disbelief. Responsible and dependable were two qualities often used to describe his character, yet Mya was treating him as if he wasn't either. Granted, she didn't know a lot about him, but he assumed with the mutual friends they shared, she knew enough.

"I've had an office in Chicago for years since I have so many clients in this city," he said enjoying the surprised look on her face. "So I'm constantly commuting anyway. Trust me, I'm a man of my word."

Mya squinted her eyes once more before the tension finally released from her face. She sat on the edge of her desk, her navy skirt rising ever so slowly up her luscious thighs. *Smooth. Creamy. Kissable.* In any other situation with an attractive woman, Malik would have kept his eyes positioned on the woman's face. After all, he was a trained private investigator who usually portrayed patience and discipline.

But Mya wasn't just any woman and after listening to the incorrect judgments she'd made about his character since he stepped into her office, he figured he was allowed to take a look at the sexy set of legs he'd love to see wrapped around his midsection.

When the room grew silent with awareness, Malik forced himself to tear his gaze away from her to peer at the clock on the wall.

"I have to get going, but I'm in town for the next few days. How about we meet up and discuss some of the details for the charity date auction over dinner. I want to make sure I'm giving you exactly want you need," Malik said, purposefully implying a double meaning. She couldn't mask the interest reflected in her eyes quickly enough, proving to Malik that she could feel their chemistry as well. But he also knew that she would refuse to entertain the idea unless he gave her a push in the right direction.

"I could pick you up around seven and we could head to that Spanish restaurant in the West Loop," he continued. During Cyd and Shawn's rehearsal dinner, he'd heard Mya mention to Lex that she had really been enjoying Spanish food lately. He wasn't sure if that was still the case, but he hoped it was.

She tilted her head to the side and slightly squinted her eyes in observation. "Why can't we just meet for lunch or meet here at the office?"

He sensed her hesitation, so he decided to adjust his tactic. "Tell you what," he said crossing his arms over his chest. "If you want, we can meet at my office and I'll order takeout. That way, you get to see my office and we won't be alone because my assistant will still be there finalizing some paperwork for me."

Her brow creased as she considered his suggestion. Malik forced himself to concentrate on her face and not the increased pace of her breathing that drew attention to the peaks of her breasts lightly covered in a white blouse. To him, meeting in his private office was much more intimate than meeting in a restaurant, but the choice was hers to make.

"So," he said uncrossing his arms and placing his

hands in the pockets of his sleek black slacks. "What will it be? The restaurant or my office?"

Mya met Malik's stare, determined to give him her best poker face. She knew what he was doing. If she chose the restaurant, it would feel more like a date rather than a business dinner. If she chose his office, even with his assistant there, it would probably feel more intimate than the restaurant.

She gave him a quick glance over. There was no doubt that Malik's good looks would garner more attention to the charity date auction. Especially when single hopefuls found out he would be cohosting. And she knew he really did have a lot of connections. The more people they had at the auction and the more prominent singles that agreed to be auctioned off, the better turnout they would have.

She didn't need help with the planning portion because most of it was already under control. But she did need someone who was reliable and believed in the cause. She didn't doubt that Malik had the best intentions, but she had hoped he would back out when he realized she didn't want to work with him. Instead, it only made him try harder.

She had to give him points for his patience. The past few minutes, he had been silently awaiting her answer and she hadn't done much talking after her rant about him cohosting.

She took a deep breath and thought about her choices once more. Standing before her in that sexy suit and those glasses, he reminded her of Tyson Beckford on this reality show she'd watched a few weeks ago, and it wasn't making her decision to constantly reject him an easy one.

"Okay," she said as she stood from her desk. She slightly smiled to herself over the fact that he was trying his best not to look at her legs and thighs as she did so. Her heels gave her an extra three inches, but at about six feet tall he still towered over her five-foot-three-inch frame. "How about you give me the address to your office and I'll meet you there on Thursday."

His lips curled into a slow smile. "Sounds like a plan. As promised, I'll order dinner while we work. I'll stick with Spanish if that's okay with you."

"Spanish is fine," she replied, moving behind her metal and glass desk. She pulled a business card from the desk holder and jotted down her personal cell number on the back. "If you don't already have it, here's my contact information in case anything changes with your schedule."

"No, I didn't have it. Thank you, but I doubt anything will change," he said with confidence as he took the card from her before slipping his own business card out of his pants pocket. "Here is the address to my Chicago office," he said, jotting down the information on the back of the card. Just as she'd carefully given her card to him, she was cautious to accept his card without their hands touching.

"This is the address," she stated as she read the details he'd written on the back of the card since the front had his Detroit information. "It's only a few minutes away from here and right down the street from Micah and Shawn's office."

He gave her a small grin before responding. "It's

definitely the right address. I was the one who told Micah and Shawn about the River North vacancy. But I wasn't aware that the Elite Events office was this close until today."

"Then I guess it's just my luck that you're so close to my office," she said sarcastically.

"Do you ever think about the things you say before you say them?"

She smiled pretentiously. "Of course I do. Some people just take what I say the wrong way." Mya was a straight shooter and she'd rather be blunt and honest with people than passive and misleading.

"If you say so," Malik said with a slight laugh. "But something tells me you've been asked that before."

She shrugged her shoulders and pretended to tidy a few unruly papers on her desk. He was right. She had been asked that question before. But she wouldn't dare tell him that. He already seemed to pick up on more of her personality traits than any man she'd met before.

She was still fumbling with the papers when she chanced a look in his direction. As she'd predicted, his eyes were still locked on her. But it wasn't the look in his eyes that was unnerving her at the moment. It was the slow curl of his lips when he caught her attention.

Oh lord, what is he thinking? Mya wasn't the type to ever put much effort forth into trying to figure out what a man was thinking. But she also never really cared since for the most part, men were always really easy for her to read.

In her experience, there were two thoughts that

men always had on their mind regardless of the conversation or situation. The most obvious thought was always how soon they could get laid, and the less recognizable thought that was still true of most men, was the process of trying to remember everything about you so they could masturbate later to the vision of having sex with you.

Both thoughts had been proven true on more than one occasion. Men dreamed of situations with women they knew would never happen in real life. Nevertheless, it didn't stop some men from trying to pursue the object of their desire any chance they got. She had no doubt that Malik wanted to sleep with her since they had obvious chemistry. She could admit that the thought of sleeping with him had crossed her mind more than once, but Malik wasn't like most men. He kept his thoughts more guarded. And the reason she assumed they always got caught staring at one another was because neither one of them could ever really tell what the other was thinking.

Malik was very respectable and while they had only had a couple conversations, it hadn't felt forced like other men she'd been in contact with. But what annoyed Mya about Malik wasn't that she put him in the same category as most men…it was the fact that she didn't.

That smile, that side smirk that he did all too well, had a lot of meaning behind it. From what she'd observed, Malik was safe. Predictable. Played by the rules. However, when he gave her that smirk, she wasn't quite sure he was as harmless as she assumed he was.

Breaking their trance, Malik glanced at his black

metal watch and informed her that he had to get going. As he made his way to her office door, Mya stood to see him out, careful not to get too close to him.

When he reached the door, he slightly glanced over his shoulder, catching Mya off guard. "I look forward to our meeting on Thursday," he said as he studied her eyes once more, and shut the door.

As the door closed behind him, Mya placed her hand on her stomach and swished a light breath into the air. She remembered in a business class she had taken in college, her professor had stated that it was beneficial to study the competition and familiarize yourself with their strengths, weaknesses, and their sales and marketing tactics so that you could develop a strategic plan to win over a client or business.

Mya knew this wasn't exactly the same situation, but it sure as hell felt like it. Malik was up to something and she knew it had to do with her. She really didn't have any time to focus on avoiding a man's advances and a couple months ago, she thought she had succeeded in figuring out the type of man he was. But today had been an eye-opener. Although she had thought she had made herself clear in Anguilla that she had no interest in going out with him, it was obvious that Malik Madden could not be underestimated.

Chapter 3

Malik glanced around the small conference room, glad that Mona, his office manager, had cleared out the boxes that had originally been stored in the room.

"Do you need me to do anything else?" Mona asked.

"No, that's all for today," Malik responded as he opened the blinds to allow sunlight to seep into the room before the sun set.

"Great," Mona replied. "I placed an order for the food to arrive around 8:00 p.m. As promised, I'll leave now, so you can have the office to yourself. Good luck with your meeting."

"Thanks, Mona." The minute Mya had agreed to meet him at his office he had decided that he would release Mona a little early that day. He figured Mya wouldn't like that they were alone, but he definitely preferred it that way.

Malik checked the clock on the cream-colored wall before heading back to his office. *She should be here soon.* He had a feeling she was a stickler for being on time after the speech she had given him the other day about being reliable.

When he arrived to his office, he glanced around at the decor he had added to the walls. Abstract paintings created by his younger brother Malakai now decorated the once-bland space. He'd also replaced his furniture with more contemporary office furnishings. With the help of Mona, his Chicago office was finally starting to look like a place where he actually spent time.

The loud sound of the buzzer interrupted his perusal of the office.

"Madden Incorporated," Malik said into the speaker.

"Hi, Malik. It's Mya."

"I'll buzz you up." As he pressed the buzzer to let her into his second floor office, he took note of the way she had said his name. He enjoyed listening to the way his name rolled off her tongue, but the way she said it sounded too formal. This might be a professional meeting, but Malik preferred her to sound a little more relaxed.

At the light ding of the elevator, he opened the door to his office suite just as she was stepping into the hallway. She had worn a similar skirt to when he had seen her a couple days ago, but this one was beige and she wore it with a russet-colored blouse. The colors really brought out the golden highlights in her wavy brown hair that he hadn't really noticed before.

"You look great," he said. She gave him a quick

up and down glance before replying, "Thanks, so do you."

Malik had chosen to get rid of his tie and had unbuttoned the first few buttons of his light gray dress shirt that he'd paired with dark gray slacks.

"Thanks. If you'll follow me to the conference room, we can begin discussing business." Mya followed behind Malik and he could feel her eyes glued to the back of his head.

"You must be in Chicago quite a bit," she said as they passed Mona's desk.

"Not really," he replied as he held open the conference room door for her to enter. She placed her bag and purse in a nearby chair and sat down at the table, observing the art on the wall. "Since I'll be cohosting the auction and I currently have more clients in Illinois than Michigan, I figured I would work out of Chicago for a while."

Mya's head whipped towards Malik just as he took a seat across the table from her.

"You're staying in Chicago?" she asked.

"Yes, I am. I figured it would be easier than all the traveling. But once a week, I'll still take a drive to my office in Detroit. I have an office manager and three interns there, so my office is in good hands."

Mya stared at him for a while and didn't say anything. He imagined that she was still trying to accept the fact that he would be residing in her city for a while.

She cleared her throat and nervously brushed her fingers through her hair before leaning back in the swivel chair. The act was done subconsciously, which made her look even sexier to Malik. She had a good poker face. He'd give her that. But he was paid to see beneath the surface and study a person's actions. He wondered if Mya knew that her actions were proving just how nervous she was.

"So," she said, recovering from his statement. "You said your assistant would be here too. Did she step out for a minute?"

"Actually, I told her she could go home early, so it's just the two of us," he responded.

"Oh, I see," she said, her brown eyes growing slightly bigger before returning to their normal size.

He was sure she didn't see the big picture. Not fully anyway. Malik was a careful thinker. He was the type of person who could develop a plan that would take years to execute. And he would maintain his patience until every task of the plan had been completed.

"Where will you stay?" she asked.

"I own an apartment complex in Hyde Park. I have tenants in all units except the penthouse, so I will reside there while I'm in Chicago."

"Nice," she said as she began removing items from her bag. "Did you decide how long you will stay?"

I'm sure much longer than you'd like. "Probably at least until the auction. After that, I'll play it by ear."

Malik stood up and walked to the corner of the conference room where the Keurig was placed. "Would you like some coffee?"

"I don't drink coffee," she stated as she jotted something down in her notepad. "But tea would be great if you have it."

"Yes, I do," he said as he placed the sugar holder

and stirrers on the conference table. "So, how about you tell me the overall goal of the fundraiser."

"Sure," she said as she crossed one leg over the other. It took all Malik's strength not to drop his eyes to her legs. He distracted himself with making his coffee and her tea instead.

"At Elite Events, there are a variety of organizations and events that we sponsor. One of my most cherished sponsorships is the work we do with Chicago after-school programs. There are two programs in particular that we donate a hefty amount of money to annually. But a few months ago we learned that our efforts to save those programs weren't effective, and they will have to permanently close before the start of school."

"That's unfortunate," Malik responded as he placed the hot drinks on the conference table.

"Exactly," Mya stated. "After talking with my partners, we've decided to open our own after-school program. The employees who currently work in the programs that are closing have agreed to transition to our program since they will be out of jobs soon. It will take a lot of hard work to make everything happen in a little over three months, but we have a lot of support, so I think we can do it. I'll also be spending one or two days a week as needed working in the office of the after-school program instead of the Elite Events office."

"Wow," Malik stated as he absorbed everything Mya had said. "I admire your dedication, it will really make a difference in the community."

She smiled before she slid a piece of paper across the desk. "Thanks. I just hope we can help the students that benefit from the programs that are closing and also bring awareness to those who don't follow what goes on in the education system. We can't fund the entire program and keep it running without the help of the community, that's why we are having the charity date auction next month."

"I'd say you're well on your way and I like the idea of a date auction to raise money. June is a good month to have a singles event because people probably spent last fall, winter and spring preparing mentally and physically for the hot weather."

"Exactly," Mya said nodding her head in agreement. "You know the streets overflow with people as soon as the weather gets above fifty degrees. And it will take place right after school ends."

"So," Malik said as he stirred around the sugar and hazelnut cream he'd poured into his coffee. "What help do you need from me?"

"Well, that piece of paper details everything," she replied as she pointed to the paper she had slid across the table. "It's a tentative schedule of all deadlines including dates for auditions to see what singles we want to auction off and many other details. My partners and I have settled on auctioning off twenty singles…ten women and ten men. Of the twenty participants, I want at least half to be business professionals or well known individuals in the Midwest states to up the ante and get singles more excited at the possibility of going out with a local celebrity. I already have two business women and two Chicago athletes who have agreed, so I'm looking for about six more."

"I can definitely reach out to a few people as well," Malik added.

"Great! We may charge a small fee to enter the auction and since we're event planners, we will plan dates for a few lucky couples in the audience."

"How would that work?" Malik asked.

"Two weeks before the auction, we will email a questionnaire for everyone to fill out. Anyone interested in winning a date will only have forty-eight hours to fill out the form and return it to us. Then we will shuffle through the data and match at least six singles. We will announce the matches at the auction."

"It looks like you and your partners even have the media plan for the event taken care of," Malik said as he skimmed the sheet of paper.

"We do," Mya said as she nodded her head. "Which is why I knew we didn't really have to meet tonight to discuss anything further. I will let you know when I need you."

Malik laughed. *Nice try.* "That's where you're wrong, Mya."

"How so?" she asked as she scrunched her forehead.

Malik spun in his chair and reached for the red folder he'd placed aside before Mya arrived. He quickly glanced at her before removing a sheet of paper from the folder and handing it to her.

"What's this?" Mya asked, not even bothering to look down at the paper.

Malik crossed his hands in front of him on the table. "If you take a look at that document, you will notice that I need to be involved with every step of the process."

Mya yanked the paper off the table and skimmed the contents stated. "A contract? You drafted a contract? For what? You're just a cohost, so all you really need to do is support, promote and be present for any rehearsals and of course the day of the auction."

He smirked and ignored the hitch in her voice. He knew she wouldn't like the idea of working with him more than she'd planned. But she'd just have to deal with it.

"It's not a draft," he stated in a calm voice. "If you pay close attention, it's an actual contract that Lex, Imani and Cyd signed when I left your office the other day."

Mya stood from her chair and slammed the paper on the table in front of him. "I don't know what bullshit you're trying to pull, but I never signed this contract and since I'm the lead planner of the event, this isn't valid."

He shot her a sly smirk, knowing the action would make her even more upset, but he couldn't help it. He enjoyed seeing her all hot and bothered. "Quite the contrary, Mya. It clearly states in the fine print that only two members from Elite Events need to sign off on a contract."

He watched the rise and fall of her chest as she came to the realization that he had her pinned in a corner. "If you look closely," he continued as he pointed to the document, "I have three signatures, so your signature isn't needed."

She squinted her eyes at him. "Why are you doing this?" she asked him softly.

Malik studied her expression, hoping that he hadn't made a mistake by pushing her to work more closely with him. "Before I even talked to you about the charity date auction, Lex had filled me in on the efforts Elite Events were trying to make. I believe in giving back to the community and I wanted to help."

He slid an envelope to her that had Elite Events written on it. "Here, open this."

Mya looked hesitant at first, but she took the envelope and opened it. Her eyes grew big in surprise before she responded. "Is this for our after-school program?" she asked as she glanced back down at the check.

"Yes, I decided to help sponsor the date auction and I have a few more checks coming from a few business friends of mine who also want to help your cause. As you stated before, you need help if you're going to achieve this goal."

Malik watched some of her frustration subside, but he knew she still had a lot of fight left concerning his close involvement. Mya wasn't the type of woman who liked being strong-armed into anything, but he could also tell that she really cared for the Chicago students and wouldn't let her pride get in the way of helping them out.

"I need to make a call," she said as she stood up from the conference table and smoothed out her blouse. "If you'll excuse me, I'll be right back," she said before walking out of the conference room and firmly shutting the door behind her.

Malik leaned back in his seat and titled his head to the ceiling. *I wonder how long it will take her to process everything.* The food was due to arrive any minute, but he wasn't sure if he could even talk her into staying after the news he'd just dropped on her.

A part of him felt wrong for putting her in this situation, but little did she know, if they didn't seem to work well together, he would back off and let her continue preparing for the date auction alone. He truly did admire her determination to start a new afterschool program and he didn't want anything standing in the way of her achieving that…not even him.

Chapter 4

"Who the hell does he think he is?" she said through clenched teeth into the phone as she paced the hallway. "I don't care how much money he wants to donate. He can't blackmail me into working with him."

"It's hardly blackmail," Lex said on the other line. "He presented Imani, Cyd and I with an actual contract that we had our lawyer review. He isn't asking Elite Events for anything more than allowing Madden Incorporated to cosponsor the date auction and be notified of all the steps of the planning process."

"Sounds like blackmail to me since I'm the main Elite Events founder planning this event," Mya huffed.

"Mya, it's not as bad as it sounds," said another voice through the line. Mya looked questionally at her phone before bringing it back up to her ear.

"Imani, is that you?"

"Yes, it's me."

"And me," Cyd chimed in.

Mya slowly closed her eyes and dropped her head to the floor. "Let me guess, all three of you are together."

They didn't have time to answer before she heard the soft cooing of baby DJ in the background that proved her point.

"No need to answer. You all knew I was getting together with Malik tonight anyway. Ugh, this is ridiculous. I was really looking forward to planning the date auction drama-free."

"Malik is by far the least dramatic person I know," Imani responded.

"So true," Cyd agreed. "You're way more dramatic than he is. Just look at how you're reacting right now."

"I'm not even going to respond to that," Mya rebuked.

"No need. I know I'm right," Cyd replied.

"Listen," Mya said ready to start a debate. She was fed up with the entire situation.

Before she could begin, Lex cut her off. "Mya, it won't be that bad. The bottom line is, Malik is co-sponsoring the event and donating an extremely generous amount of money. If I know you, you probably didn't even read the contract in detail since your first thought was to reject whatever it stated. He isn't asking for a lot and he is nowhere near as demanding as Micah was when y'all signed off on that ridiculous contract he had drawn up for me last year."

Mya smiled as she thought about the part she'd played in the contract Micah had presented to Lex last year when he needed Elite Events' help planning an event.

The sound of the elevator ding distracted her from her call. "Hold on, guys," she said into the phone before placing them on mute.

She followed the food courier who had walked into Micah's office suite. "Hello, can I help you?"

"Sorry, someone was leaving so I came right up," the young man said with a smile. "I have a food delivery for Malik Madden."

Mya observed the restaurant icon on the brown paper bag and wondered if he'd purposely ordered food from one of her favorite Spanish restaurants. *If he did, how did he even find out?* "I can take it," she stated as she took the bag. "Hold on while I get some money for your tip."

"No need," the courier stated. "It's already been taken care of. Have a great day, miss."

"You too," she replied as he walked out the door.

She glanced at her phone and unclicked the hold button. "Hey," she said into the phone. "Did any of you happen to give Malik a rundown of all my favorite restaurants?"

Of course, they all said no, but Mya didn't know how much she believed them. She sighed into the phone. "Okay, I'm not done with you guys, but I want to speed up this meeting, so we'll finish this conversation later."

She hung up her phone and briefly contemplated taking the food, getting on the elevator and heading to her South Loop condo. But she knew that wasn't possible. Not only was her bag still in the conference room with Malik, but she also didn't want to be that rude.

Why is he being so persistent? she asked herself as

she began walking back to the conference room. She should have known that helping Micah get closer to Lex would come back to bite her in the butt. After all, Malik and Micah were brothers, and although they were opposite in personality, they probably had a lot in common, like how they chose to pursue women they were interested in.

Mya stopped walking abruptly. Malik had only officially asked her on one date, so that didn't necessarily mean he was looking for a relationship. *He wants to get a rise out of you.* That had to be it. Malik wanted to make her feel uncomfortable so she would give in and go out with him, which was absolutely out of the question.

She took a few more steps. *But you're attracted to him too, and it's been a while since you've had sex with a man that fine.* She stopped walking again, surprised at the direction of her thoughts. "This isn't like me," she mumbled under her breath as she continued her walk back to the conference room. She didn't spend time agonizing over men and the tactics they used to try and get with her. She was too fierce for that. Too independent. She'd spent too much time trying to become the person she was today and had gone through too many misfortunes to let the likes of one man jeopardize her character. She could handle this. *So what if you're more attracted to him than you are most men. Who cares!* She'd overcome a lot in her thirty years and she could definitely handle a man like Malik Madden.

When she opened the door to the conference room, Malik's back was to her as he stared out the window. It was dark outside now, but the city always looked good at night. He was positioned towards a well-lit street and he didn't appear to hear her enter. She took a brief moment to savor how good he looked from the back.

Even through his gray dress shirt, she noticed how broad and muscular his shoulders and arms were. He had unbuttoned his sleeves and rolled them to quarter length. His hands were in his pockets so his pants stretched slightly forward, accentuating his butt.

Standing there ogling him felt somewhat invasive, but she couldn't help it. It was hard enough trying to not sneak glances at him when he was watching her, so it was even harder to tear her eyes away when he didn't know she was watching.

She failed to pick up on any signs that he was turning to face her and by the time he had fully turned around, he caught her gawking at him. Despite being caught red-handed, she darted her eyes away from him, refusing to look him in the face.

"The food came," she stated as she placed the bag on the table.

"Are you okay?" he asked sincerely, the deep timbre in his voice catching her off guard. She forced herself to steal a glance in his direction and when she did, she'd instantly wished that she hadn't. *Oh, my.* He had on his glasses. The glasses that he sported better than any man she'd ever seen wear glasses. He hadn't been wearing them before she stepped out of the room so the sight of them now was even more unsettling.

He held her gaze, patiently awaiting her response.

"I'm fine," she said taking the seat she had vacated. "We can continue with the meeting."

He nodded and took his seat before he began explaining how he'd make as many meetings with the auctionees as possible.

Mya was barely listening to him. All she could think about was how in the world she would make it through him being in the same city as her. *How can I get through the next month when I can barely get through this meeting*, she thought as she sank into her chair a little.

She was screwed. Royally screwed. And it wasn't the I-can-jump-back-from-this type of screwed. It was more like the *Oh god, I will never sin again if you help me through this situation* type of screwed.

"When is the first meeting with the auctionees?" he asked, oblivious to the inner struggle she was currently experiencing.

She plastered on a fake smile before responding to his question. "Next Wednesday evening I'm meeting with the four business professionals I was telling you about."

"Great," he responded. "This weekend I should hear from a couple people I reached out to as well. If they accept, can I invite them to the meeting?"

"Sure, that would work. I hope to have a few more people solidified by the first meeting too," she replied as she glanced at the bag of food she'd placed on the conference table. "How about we take a break to eat."

"Sounds good," Malik replied with a smirk. "My office manager stored some paper plates, plastic utensils and cold water in the kitchenette. I'll get those and be right back."

"Okay," she said as Malik got up and left the conference room. She reached for the brown paper bag and began taking out the containers of food. Although she had originally thought that the time leading up to the auction would fly by, there was no doubt in her mind that it couldn't come soon enough now.

Mya connected her iPhone to her Bluetooth speaker and placed both devices on the countertop of her white marble sink. As a soft and slow melody from Jill Scott filled the bathroom with sweet sounds of relaxation, she slipped out of her plush white robe and twirled her wavy brown hair atop her head before securing it with a clip.

Seeing Malik a couple days ago and finding out that she would be seeing a lot more of him had been something completely unexpected. Mya could usually handle pressure very well, but over the past few months, it seemed that someone in the universe was playing a cruel joke on her.

She'd been so excited to land a great venue for the date auction right after she had discussed the idea with her partners. But a call she'd received earlier today had been full of disappointing news. Not only had the venue been accidently double booked, but her second option wasn't available either. Between trade shows, bridal shows, job fairs and people in town for summer events, marathons and festivals, the best venues in Chicago and Chicagoland were booked solid the day of the date auction. It was too late to change the date, so she had to find another solution, and quickly since the event was in three weeks. It would be difficult enough just to change the location but now she would also have to find a hotel close to the new venue for out-of-town attendees.

Mya turned off the water of her stand-alone

wrought-iron tub and dipped her toes in the water to test the heat level. Deciding it was the perfect temperature for a relaxing bath, she slowly eased her body into the hot water and leaned her head against a soft white pillow.

"Much better," she said aloud to herself as she softly closed her eyes. This had been the most relaxing thing she'd done in the past few days and her eucalyptus bath oil with a hint of sweet jasmine was the perfect aroma to calm her nerves.

She'd also received a voicemail once she left her meeting with Malik from one of the business professionals saying that she could no longer participate due to family obligations, but still planned on donating. Mya had been extremely disappointed because the natural-hair icon was very well known and respected in the Chicago community—especially in the beauty industry. Her presence would have gotten the attention of a lot of beauty professionals and she hoped she was able to find a replacement that would draw the same type of crowd.

The light ding of her phone caused her to open her eyes. "What is it now?" she said to herself, expecting some more bad news regarding the auction. She lifted a wet manicured hand out of the tub and gently patted away some of the moisture with a towel before reaching for her phone. She was surprised to see that it wasn't additional bad news about the auction, but instead, a reminder that she'd set for herself last month.

"Time is ticking. You need to decide how to handle the call," she read aloud. "Hmm." She knew exactly what call she had been referring to. Mya put her phone back down and slid even deeper into the tub.

She was never the type to prolong decisions that had to be made and had always been a decisive person. Except when it came to this call or dealing with any decisions that she had to make about her past. When it came to those types of choices, she could procrastinate for an extremely long amount of time.

But procrastinating never solved anything. The person who had called her a few months ago had claimed to know about her birth mother. A mother who Mya had never gotten the chance to know and who, according to hints from the caller, had passed away.

"Why now?" she yelled into the air as she tilted her head to the ceiling. Growing up, Mya had always dreamed that her mother would one day show up to whatever foster home she was at, claim she never meant to give her up and take her to her home. But that had only been foolish thinking on Mya's part. When she became a teenager, she realized that she was given up for a reason, so the odds of her mother suddenly deciding that she wanted to have her in her life were slim to none.

But still, it was important to know where you came from and who you came from. Mya knew that any contact from someone who might know about her past was something she needed to consider researching further.

Her eyes drifted closed again as her thoughts wandered to Malik. She was an extremely private person and her partners knew not to push her to discuss anything about her past that she didn't freely want to discuss. Malik didn't know anything about her beyond Mya, the successful event planner who was passionate about after-school programs. He had only seen her in business settings or friendly gatherings with people who had known her long enough in her adulthood not to question her life as an adolescent. But he didn't know the other side of her. The side she often kept concealed from the outside world. The Mya who didn't have a family of her own to visit on the holidays. The Mya who had worked four jobs at age sixteen to save up for a better life when other girls were going out on dates and getting a weekly allowance from their parents.

But Malik is a private investigator, a little voice inside her head echoed. *If you let him, he could probably help you.* Her eyes quickly opened when she thought about what confiding in Malik would mean. She had never relied on anyone for help and it didn't matter if it was his job or not, trusting Malik was completely out of the question.

You're just scared you'll find out more than you bargained for. She shot upright and braced both hands on either side of the tub, expecting to see a face belonging to the voice inside her head. Sometimes, her thoughts were so powerful that they caught her off guard. Mya had never been afraid of anything. She couldn't afford to be. And if she had been, she had deliberately hid her fears, even to herself sometimes. But as she stared out into the empty space in the bathroom, she knew the voice inside her head was speaking the words she wouldn't dare say out loud. Words that continued to float through her mind as she slipped back into the tub and tried her best to relax.

Chapter 5

"Is everything okay with her?" Winter Dupree, Malik's cousin and the owner of Bare Sophistication lingerie boutique asked.

Malik glanced over at Mya who was sporting a chic pantsuit and discussing a few of the date auction details with one of the business professionals. He hadn't seen her since last week and had traveled to Detroit over the weekend. He hoped she wasn't still upset about the contract.

"I'm not sure," he said to his cousin as he observed the strained smile Mya wore. After she'd called him a couple days ago and informed him that one of their prospects for the auction could no longer participate, he'd quickly called his cousin and asked if she wanted to be a part of the charity date auction. It had only taken a little coaxing to get her to agree since she had only been residing in Chicago for a year and never passed on an opportunity to represent Bare Sophistication and network.

"Well, I suggest you find out," Winter said as she placed her hand on his shoulder. "I don't know Mya well, but I have a feeling her bark is worse than her bite. Find out what's going on in that head of hers." She gave him a soft smile before walking over to Mya to bid her goodbye. Once they were alone, the silence in the Elite Events conference room was deafening.

"Do you want to talk about anything?" he asked as he helped her straighten up.

"I'm fine," she stated as she picked up her folder and notes from the meeting without making eye contact. "I'd say that meeting went well, don't you think?"

"Yes, it went extremely well. Any news on finding another venue for the event?"

"I'm working on it," she said finally looking at him and giving him a half smile. "We may have to settle for a mediocre venue since all the great places have been taken, but I'm sure we could transform whatever place we choose into something great. As of now, we are telling the public that the location is secret and will be disclosed closer to the event to add suspense. It's actually working and our social media followers are increasing by the day."

"That's good news," Malik said with a smile. "Great plan."

"Thanks." Mya pushed in the final office chair. "Well, I guess that's all for tonight. And I wanted to apologize for not thanking you last week. I really appreciate the donation."

"You're welcome," he replied as he leaned against

the doorjamb and crossed his arms over his chest. "I'm happy to donate to the cause and I'm confident that everything will work out and the auction will be a success."

He was fishing for a sign that her mood had to do with the auction since it didn't appear that she was going to willingly tell him what was wrong.

"Oh, I'm confident everything will turn out great with the auction," she stated as she clutched the folder and notepad to her chest. He studied the worry lines etched across her face and the droop of her mouth. *Something else is bothering her.* And from the looks of it, he suspected that whatever was bothering her had been bothering her for a while, although he couldn't be sure.

He expected her to eventually look away from him, but instead, she kept her eyes locked on his. She shuffled her feet, bringing his attention to her body language. By the way she was standing, she appeared standoffish and unapproachable. Though her eyes didn't mirror her mannerisms. Her eyes seemed to plea for something, but he wasn't quite sure what that something was. *Help? Advice?*

"Are you busy tonight?" he asked, breaking the silence.

"No," she answered as she nodded her head.

Malik moved away from the doorjamb and stepped closer to her. "I was going to take a walk along the lake to watch the fireworks at Navy Pier. Would you like to join me?"

Her facial expression hadn't changed, but he took note that the rise and fall of her chest had quickened.

"Sure," she replied. "Let me just put this stuff in my office and get my things."

"Okay," Malik said as he followed her to her office, careful not to seem too surprised that she'd accepted his offer.

After Mya had locked up the office and Malik had signed out of the visitor log for the building, they both stepped out into the crisp spring air.

"Are we driving or walking?" she asked.

Malik looked up at the night sky before checking the weather app on his phone to make sure it wasn't going to rain. "Let's walk and I'll walk you back to your car after the fireworks."

She nodded her head in agreement and they began walking in comfortable silence towards the lake. The temperature had dropped, but he welcomed the night breeze. He looked over at Mya who was looking straight ahead, her face void of emotion. He figured she was thinking about whatever had been on her mind earlier in her office.

"I hear this is a great spot to sit," he said as he pointed to a wooden bench.

Mya glanced around the area. "Usually all the good places to view the fireworks are swarming with people. How did you find one of the few secluded places when you don't even permanently live here?"

"My brother told me," he said with a chuckle. "I guess he figured I needed something to do tonight and he knows I don't like crowds of people."

"Ahh," Mya said, finally giving him a smile.

"There it is," he said as they reached the bench and sat beside one another.

"There what is?" Mya asked.

Malik adjusted his suit jacket and glanced to his side at Mya. "There's that smile I've been waiting to see all evening."

"Oh, boy," she said with a laugh as she lightly punched him in his shoulder. "That was so corny."

He flashed her his pearly whites. "But it made you laugh so I'd say I'm two for two tonight."

She laughed again as she pushed aside dark brown tendrils of hair that had blown in her face. "Whatever you say, Malik."

They both leaned back on the bench and turned to face the lake. Malik was glad that the area where they were seated didn't have any bright lights. It was lit just enough for them to see one another and their surroundings. He could hear the light hum of passing conversations from other spectators who also knew about his secluded area and awaited the fireworks presentation.

"Sometimes, at the end of the day, I walk to the lake and watch the sunset," Mya said.

"Seems really relaxing."

"It is. I do some of my best thinking during those times."

"I bet," he responded as he stretched out his legs and crossed one ankle over the other. "I've always preferred being alone with my thoughts instead of surrounded by people asking me what I think."

"I'm quite the opposite," Mya replied. "Sort of."

"What do you mean?"

"Well, everyone needs that alone time to think," she stated as she crossed one leg over the other. "But I don't mind being surrounded by people and having someone to talk to or bounce ideas off of. Unfortunately, I don't like answering questions about my thoughts, so that's why I sort of agree with you and at the same time, I kinda don't."

Okay, so she's really sociable, yet private at the same time. Me too. "Then I guess it's best that I don't ask you what types of things you think about when you watch the sunset," he said jokingly. She laughed along with him.

"I enjoy bouncing ideas off of others too, but growing up with five brothers meant there was never any private time, so I learned to cherish the alone time I had."

"That's understandable," Mya said. Malik waited for her to expand, but she didn't appear to have anything else to add.

"Did you ever wish you had more alone time when you were growing up?" Malik asked. She didn't answer right away.

"I was always surrounded by kids, but I often felt alone," she said a little quieter than before. "I did make a couple friends in foster care at a couple homes, but I bounced around so much that it was often hard to forge lasting relationships."

Foster care? "I had no idea you grew up in foster care," he responded, surprised that he hadn't heard anything about it from his brother.

"Hmm, I bet it changes your image of me now, doesn't it?" she said, turning her head in his direction. He didn't miss the negative tone in her voice as she spoke.

"What makes you say that?"

"Well, I'm sure you didn't think this amazingly

well-rounded and educated woman grew up in foster care."

Ah, I see. "You assume that's what I think?" Malik asked. "Did I miss the memo that growing up in foster care somehow meant you were less likely to be well-rounded and educated?"

"It's not about your upbringing, but rather the person you decide you want to be," she huffed.

"I agree with that statement," Malik said as he pointed to himself. "But evidently you think differently based off the fact that you assume your upbringing matters to me," he continued as he pointed to her.

"I don't expect you to understand the type of person I am."

"I really won't understand if you choose to hide the type of person you are and pretend to be someone you're not."

"What is that supposed to mean?" she asked, her voice raising a notch. "I've always been real with people and if they don't accept me, that's their problem, not mine."

"That may be the case," Malik said, keeping his voice in the same octave. "I know a little about the woman you are now and she seems amazing, but opening up about the person you used to be or the life you used to have isn't a bad thing. People pass judgment about things they don't understand. You've never bothered to ask me anything about myself, so you really don't know what type of person I am or what I understand. Yet you've passed judgment on me, questioned my character and now you've accused me of being judgmental."

"Oh great," she said sarcastically. "I guess now

is the time we share childhood sob stories while we hold hands and sing 'Kumbaya.'" Malik blinked a few times and gave her a blank stare. *Micah wasn't lying...her tongue is lethal.* And despite the way she was using that tongue to give him a verbal lashing, he was still curious to know how it would feel to put her tongue to better use. Preferably something that required little speaking and more mouth-to-mouth action.

"I'm not sure how this conversation escalated, but it wasn't my plan to force you to talk to me when I invited you to watch the fireworks," Malik stated. "Back in the office, I thought you needed a break. That's all."

She held his stare for a few seconds before rubbing her neck with the palm of her hand and looking back to the lake. He'd hoped to cheer her up, but it seemed his presence was having the opposite affect.

When she looked at him again, he expected her to make up an excuse to return to her car and call it a night. Instead, she said three words he didn't expect to hear.

"Maybe you're right," she said faintly. "As I said before, I don't really share much about myself with people, but tonight, I knew I needed to talk to you."

Malik scooted closer to her on the bench so that he could hear her better. "What do you need to talk to me about?" he asked.

She bit her bottom lip and fumbled with her fingers, the act appearing vulnerable and endearing to Malik.

"I need to hire you," she stated. "To investigate something for me."

She's nervous. "Of course I'll help you," he said without question. "What do you need me to investigate?"

She took a deep breath and closed her eyes. When she opened them, emotion and confusion were written all across them. "Before Cyd and Shawn's wedding I received a call from a woman who claimed to know my birth mother. She called me privately and I don't know how she found me. I was too much in shock to ask her any details although I know I should have at least tried to see if she would answer…"

"What did she say?" Malik asked after she hesitated.

"Well, I always knew I was left at a church when I was a baby with a note that only had the name *Mya* written on it, so I've never known anything about my family." She blew out a frustrated breath. "I don't know who this woman is or if she's even telling me the truth, but she called to tell me that even though my mother left me, she loved me very much."

Malik watched her eyes grow dark with anger and all he wanted to do was reach out and pull her to him. But Mya didn't need his affection right now. She needed to get her story out and based off her body language, he doubted she'd voiced the words aloud to any other individual.

"My first thought was the fact that the woman said loved and not love, so that leads me to believe that maybe the woman who gave birth to me is deceased." Mya flicked some hair over her shoulder and sat up straighter on the bench. "Then my second thought was if I could recover from the hurt and disappointment if what the woman said weren't true."

The loud boom of the first fireworks brought their attention to the night sky as both gazed up at the bright lights dashing into the atmosphere. "What did she tell you?" Malik asked, looking to her as she continued to watch the fireworks display.

"She told me something that a part of me wishes she hadn't because I have a very low tolerance for people playing with my emotions." Mya turned her head back to Malik. "According to this woman, I wasn't my birth mother's only child... I have a sibling."

Chapter 6

There, I said it. Not only had Mya asked for Malik's help, but she'd also finally gotten the confidence to say the words *I have a sibling* out loud.

She was overwhelmed by the possibility that she might have a sibling. But even more nervous of having Malik investigate her life, in fear he would find things she wasn't sure she wanted to know.

She had spent her entire life trying to convince herself that the way her life had turned out was for the better. Because of her struggles, she'd built a solid life for herself. And since she didn't know anything about her biological parents, she'd grown to realize that giving her away might have actually been the best decision for them.

But sometimes, in rare moments, the shadows of her past mingled with the present, causing her to question truth from the false reality she'd created in her mind. Success didn't hide the demons battling in her subconscious and if she were honest with herself, she'd admit that the only way to slay her fears was to figure out the truth once and for all.

Malik hadn't stopped observing her since she'd made the last statement and he hadn't said a word let alone made a sound in the past couple minutes.

"Will you still help me?" she asked, unable to take the silence anymore.

"Of course I will," he replied without hesitation. "There are just a few details that I will need from you first, so we can talk about it another night if you want."

She nodded her head. "No, it's fine. We can talk now if that's okay."

"That's fine." He pulled a small notepad and pen from his suit jacket. After he tapped a button on his phone's screen, turning on a flashlight, he began jotting down notes. Mya assumed he was writing what he'd found out from her so far and she wished she could make out the words from where she sat beside him.

"And I assume you'll also let me know how much it costs for your personal services," she stated as she squinted in the darkness and placed her hand on his thigh trying to lean in to read the notepad.

When he stopped moving his hands, she glanced up and found him looking at her intently with one eyebrow raised. His eyes left her face and slowly fell to his thigh.

"I'm sorry," she said as she moved her hand and jumped back from him.

"No apology necessary," he said as he continued to jot down notes. "I just want to be clear. What personal services are you referring to?"

"Really," she said sarcastically. "Obviously, I'm talking about your investigator services."

"Okay. As for my services, they'll be free of charge. I'd like to think we are starting to actually become friends and I made a commitment years ago that, depending on the circumstance, I wouldn't charge friends." He stopped taking notes and turned his head towards her.

Mya forced herself to maintain eye contact, although deep down, she realized that Malik now knew more about her than most of the people in her life. She hadn't discussed the call with anyone, not even her partners.

"This is my first time confiding in anyone about this," she said without thinking. *Why the heck did I just tell him that?* Calm. Reserved. Composed. That's the Mya that everyone knew when it came to serious situations. Fidgety. Nervous. Letting words slip. Who was this woman? She was definitely not herself.

"Which brings me to my second set of services," Malik said breaking her thoughts. *Second set of services? Lord tell me he isn't talking about what I think he's talking about.*

"Second set?" she asked.

"Yes, second set," he repeated, barely appearing to blink. His voice grew deeper…more raspy. "I usually never mix business with pleasure, but if you need my intimate attention too, I'd be willing to bend the rules for you."

Mya swallowed. Hard. "I think I'm okay," she replied.

"You think or you know?"

"I know."

Malik's eyes dropped to her lips. "I think that you think you know, but you aren't really sure."

She let out a chuckle. "I think that you want to think that I'm not sure because you're hoping that I change my mind."

He lifted his eyes back to her face. "Nope, wrong again." He leaned in closer to her, his eyes floating from her lips, to her eyes, back to her lips, then up to her eyes.

Oh no, Mya thought as her heart began pounding profusely. *I wonder if he is going to try to kiss me.* When he leaned even closer to her, the question was no longer *if*, but instead, *when*.

"You will change your mind," he stated confidently. Mya racked her brain, searching for a comeback, but her mind went blank of retaliating words. Her eyes dropped to his lips as she admired their shape. His upper and bottom lip had the perfect combination of shape and fullness. She didn't know if she was so drawn to him because she hadn't been with a man in over eight months or if it was because finally deciding to investigate the call had been the most relief she'd felt in a long time. Or maybe it was because she was attracted to him no matter how hard she tried to fight it.

She barely heard the fireworks finale in the background over the fireworks going off in her stomach as his lips made their descent to hers. He was a couple centimeters away when two dings filled the air, causing him to pause. Mya wanted him to continue with the moment since she wasn't sure she would be so willing to let him kiss her again. Apparently reading her thoughts, Malik's lips ventured to hers once again.

Ding. Ding. Ding. Ding. The sounds of incoming texts messages from both their phones broke the trance.

"This better be important," Malik said as he lifted his phone to view the messages. Simultaneously Mya removed hers from her clutch.

"What!" they both said in unison as they read the messages in the group text.

"I really hate that so many of us have iPhones. These group messages seem to go on all night," Malik said. "And is it just me, or does Lex compose the longest bridal party messages known to mankind?"

"She sure does," Mya agreed as she confirmed her attendance to the bridal party meeting that had been called. "Since she wants us all to meet up, I bet she needs to make sure we are all aware of the details since their wedding will be here before you know it."

"I guess," Malik said as he put his phone in his pocket. "Since Cyd and Shawn had a short engagement, and Micah and Lex's engagement is even shorter, I didn't really think about the fact that two weddings in the same year meant twice as many wedding duties."

Mya shook her head with a laugh. "Men have no clue sometimes. I knew the minute they settled on their dates that having two friends get married the same year was going to be crazy."

Malik shrugged and joined her laughter. "Good thing you ladies are event planners."

"Very true," Mya agreed again.

Malik looked out into the lake enjoying how the moonlight reflected off the water. "That was a nice fireworks display, huh?" he asked changing the subject.

"Um, yeah," Mya said glancing at the stars in the sky. "It was really nice."

"Nice spot to view them too, right?"

"It was," she said with a smile.

"So," Malik said as he rubbed the palms of his hands against his pants. "Any chance we can pick up where we left off?"

"Not a chance," she replied with a laugh. "But I'll let you walk me to my car."

He gave her a sideways glance that made her laugh even harder. By the time she had stopped laughing, he was still shaking his head at her.

"Thanks for tonight," Mya said as they started walking in the direction of her car. She was glad she'd chosen to drive instead of taking the bus. She didn't doubt that he would have offered to take her home had she taken public transportation and she probably would have let him since it was so late.

"You're welcome," Malik said, walking beside her. They walked in comfortable silence the rest of the way to her car. It was the most relaxed she'd felt around a man in a very long time.

"You never asked me the additional questions about the call," she said when they got closer to the parking garage.

Malik gave her a lopsided smirk. "Guess that means we'll have to set up another date."

Malik took a swig of his beer and grazed his fingers over the top of the remaining cards in his hands and met Mya's stare. They only had three plays left and there was no way they were letting Shawn and Cyd take the win, especially after they were the bidders leading the current round.

Lex and Micah's bridal party get-together had resulted in the most intense game of spades he'd ever played. After eliminating two other teams, it was down to him and Mya versus Shawn and Cyd.

He reached for a card that he knew wouldn't win the hand and flicked the card in the middle of the table. He hoped that Mya had the card he was looking for and after Shawn had played his card, he was more hopeful that Mya held the winner. He kept his composure when she didn't throw out the card he was looking for.

"Oh, that sucks for y'all. You would have done better letting us take the lead this round," Cyd said as she threw down the winning card and collected the winning book. "Word of advice, Malik, Mya absolutely hates to lose. So for your sake, I hope y'all beat us."

He knew those chances were slim to none when Cyd threw out another winning card. "It looks like you're about to become public enemy number one," Cyd said as she collected another winning book.

It was down to the last round and Malik knew he didn't have the winning card, but the daggers Mya shot his way didn't really worry him. When they had defeated the first team they played, he had known that Mya was a sore loser when they had lost one round. What worried him more than dealing with Mya was the fact that Lex and Micah had repercussions for all the card losers. Their to-do list for the bridal party was longer than any list he'd ever seen and with Mya being the maid of honor and him being the best man, the stakes were high because they already had a full plate.

Malik felt a bead of sweat form on his brow as he thought about all the outstanding plans for the date auction that was two weeks away. After a well-known Chicago journalist posted an interview with Mya on her blog a day after their first meeting with the auctionees, word spread that Elite Events was still looking for a few more professional singles for the event. And they had been able to solidify the final two remaining spots that morning. But they still hadn't found another venue and time was not on their side.

"If we lose this, I'm going to hurt you," Mya said between clenched teeth. Malik didn't have to look up from the lone card in his hand to know every man in the room was laughing under their breath, assuming he would be the victim of a verbal lashing from Mya.

When Cyd played her final card, Malik tossed his card in the middle of the table, crossed his hands in front of him and looked intently at Mya. He'd observed her last couple plays, so he knew she didn't have the winning card. As predicted, Cyd threw out her last card and won.

"Game. Set. Match," Cyd said as her and Shawn stood up to do a victory hand slap across the table. Malik was barely paying attention to them because his eyes were drawn to Mya's mouth as she let out a sigh and swiped her tongue across her lips.

"You lost the game for us," she said as she crossed her arms over her chest. His eyes went back to hers.

"Yes, I did," Malik said as he continued to hold her stare.

"We didn't have to take that hand," she stated with disappointment.

"No. We didn't," Malik agreed. He could feel all eyes watching their exchange and he figured she did too since she glanced around the room before looking back at him.

"You know I don't like to lose."

"So I've heard," he said with a laugh. "So next time we compete in a game of spades, I'm going to need you to give me more help. I can't be winning all the rounds."

She blinked a couple times before giving him a sly smile. "What makes you think I'll ever agree to be on your team again?" Mya asked as she leaned over the table. "I don't play with losers or men that play too reckless. I would have thought that Ivy League education would have made you a better card player."

"Here she goes," Micah coughed.

"I don't play with women who claim to be risk takers, but sit back while I take all the risks. What happened to mutual support?" Malik leaned in even closer to her before responding. "And I don't think you'll be on my team again, I know you will." It didn't matter that Mya had a reputation for bringing a man to his knees with just one word. He wasn't just any man and she had to realize that. "You wouldn't be able to resist my charm anyways," he egged her on.

Malik loved a challenge and right now, the biggest challenge he was facing was forcing himself not to pull her across the table and kiss her next words off her lips. Mya must have sensed the direction of his thoughts because her eyes dropped to his lips before she gave him a flirtatious smile.

"You couldn't handle me, Malik," she stated a little softer than before. "I'm sure you're more used to those soft-spoken and submissive *do whatever you say* kind of women. You know, like that socially awkward uptight woman I heard you used to date. The one with zero personality."

A chorus of *ohhh*s filled the room, but Malik kept his poker face. He wondered if Mya knew that bringing up his ex was more revealing than anything else she could have said. He'd never had much interaction with Mya before, so she had to have asked about him to learn about his ex.

"I'm flattered you've been asking around about me. But see, that's were you're wrong," Malik said pointing a finger at her. "I like my women feisty and unpredictable."

"Oh, really," she said with a laugh.

"Yes, baby," Malik said shaking his head. "She has to keep me on my toes."

"I'm not your baby," she said firmly with a smile in place.

"Minor detail," he replied. "And who says being submissive to a man sometimes is a bad thing."

"Oh, I don't know," Mya said as she raised her arms into the air. "How about every independent woman in the world."

"Wrong again," he said. "If a woman has to be submissive in her values, beliefs, dreams and aspirations, then it's definitely not an ideal relationship." He brought his voice lower. "But the intimate part of the relationship should be more give and take. It's okay for a woman to be submissive in her desires, fantasies and innermost thoughts *if* the man is equally willing to surrender to her."

He expected her to retaliate right away, but she didn't. Instead, she looked at him through curious eyes, appearing to let his words sink in.

"That was really poetic, Malik," she said as she gently brushed her hand against his, the contact catching him off guard. She lightly grabbed the collar of his button-up and pulled him closer to her, bringing her lips to his ear. "But if you think a few romantic words will make me forget how terribly you lost this game for us, then obviously you don't know me very well."

He laughed when she released his collar. "Why are you always so difficult?" No matter what she said, it was obvious that the words he'd voiced before had caught her by surprise.

She feigned a look of innocence. "But I thought you liked feisty and unpredictable women," she said as she placed both hands over her heart.

"Good to see you were paying attention," he said with a grin. "Maybe next time we play together you'll use some of that spunk to intimidate the other team rather than shoot me death stares when you think we may lose."

"Whatever," she said sitting back in her seat. "We won't be losing any more games. I can't stand losing."

As Mya directed her attention to Cyd, Malik wondered if she had any idea she'd just implied that they would be playing together again.

"Well, I'll be damned," Shawn said looking from Mya to Malik. "I guess you'll live to fight another day."

Chapter 7

"Come on," she pleaded to her curling iron as she waited for the device to heat up. She checked the time on her cell phone for the third time in the past few minutes. She had to be ready in ten minutes and she still hadn't added the curls to her hair that had been on her agenda to do all morning.

After losing the spades bridal battle over the weekend, everyone in the bridal party, with the exception of the winners, had been given a plain white envelope with duties and instructions printed on a sheet of paper.

One of her many duties was to drive to a bakery in Wisconsin not far from the Illinois border on Tuesday when she still had so many things to take care of for the auction. But when she called the bakery owner, she had the great idea to ask them if they could offer any goodies for the auction. So a one-person trip turned into a duo when she asked Malik if he wanted to take some time away from the office and accompany her. If she had to be forced to keep him updated on the auction, he could at least help share the responsibilities. At least, that's the reason she told herself.

Since she didn't have time to curl her entire head, she opted for throwing a few curls in random places to add volume. Her light makeup routine was already complete so the only step she had left was to throw on the casual white summer dress she paired with a slim teal belt and matching teal sandals.

They agreed to take Malik's SUV as opposed to Mya's car, so he also decided to pick her up. She did a once-over in her large bedroom mirror before picking up her purse and the notes she had for the wedding and the date auction. When she heard her buzzer ring, she knew it was Malik. She quickly turned off all the lights before speaking into the intercom that she would head down to meet him and then she locked her door.

She'd had a lot of friends over to her home before, but Malik wasn't just any friend. He was a friend she was really attracted to and a friend who would soon know more about her past before even she did.

When she got off the elevator, she didn't see him right away. As she got closer to the door, she spotted him in the turnabout of her building leaning against his SUV wearing khaki shorts, a white polo and white gym shoes. She'd never seen him look so casual before and she knew she could definitely get used to this look.

His well-built arms were in the pockets of his shorts and he was staring at the street, oblivious to her approaching him. She slowed her steps so that she could admire him for a little while longer. *Good lawd.* The man's profile was just as sexy as his frontal stance. His strong jaw line, angular nose and nicely shaped lips were features that she'd instantly noticed when she had first met Malik. She missed his glasses today, but without them, she would be able to focus on other details in his facial features that she hadn't quite noticed before.

Over the weekend, she'd observed a slight after-five shadow and today she saw the outlines of a well-lined goatee that spanned the length of his jawline and symmetrical cheekbones. His overall physique appeared strong and fit without being overly muscular, while his skin glistened a slight shade or two darker due to the approaching summer heat. His looks were the perfect combination of rugged and sophisticated.

When she was almost near him, he finally turned toward her and mirrored the friendly smile she wore.

"Good morning," he said as he quickly admired her outfit before opening the passenger side car door.

"Good morning," she replied as she slid in the seat and noticed two cups in the cup holders. "Are one of these cups for me?" she asked when he sat in the driver's seat.

"Yes, it's tea from the café down the street." He pointed to the cup closest to the passenger seat and grabbed a small bag from the backseat. "And here's a bagel in case you're hungry now. I also packed a cooler of water and a few snacks for us."

"Guess you've thought of everything," she said.

She then smiled at the fact that he had remembered she was a tea drinker and didn't care for coffee. "But the drive is only two hours, right?"

"It is, but the GPS said it's more like two and a half to three hours in traffic. We should be there between noon and one."

"Thanks for the tea, bagel and snacks," Mya said as she took a sip of the hot tea.

"You're welcome," he said glancing over at her. "So I was wondering, do you want to chat a little more about the investigation on the drive up?"

Mya stopped sipping her tea. "We can talk about it today. I know you need to get started."

"I do," he replied as he got on the expressway. "Beginning with the number that called you. You mentioned it was private."

"Yes, she called me on a private number on my work cell, which is why I almost didn't answer. But sometimes, my clients call me privately so I answered."

"That won't be a problem," Malik said. "Even when people call from a blocked number, there is always a way to track the call. I'll just need your phone for a few hours."

"Okay," she replied finally taking another sip of her tea. "What else do you need to know? There isn't much to tell you that I haven't already. The call wasn't really long."

Malik looked to her before looking back at the road. "Sometimes, people assume that they remember everything but when they retell the story, they leave out details that they may have deemed unimportant."

"I see. That makes sense, but I was in shock, so who knows what else I know."

"Well, you've already given me a clue that you hadn't before."

She looked to him although his eyes remained on the road. "And what might that be?"

"The caller called your work cell, not your personal cell. Your work cell is listed publically somewhere, right?"

Mya thought about all the different documents and advertisements that her work cell was listed on. "That's right. And I give out that number if a client calls the main office number and asks to speak to me directly."

"Then I assume that the caller found you through your job, not by your name."

Mya's eyes briefly dropped to her lap, before she lifted her head again.

"What is it?" Malik asked. She placed her tea back in the cup holder.

"You're right, there's no way the caller could've located me by my name."

"Why's that?"

Mya let out a big sigh. "I'm confident my birth mother or parents named me Mya because the only thing that the pastor of the church found with me when I was left at the doorstep was a piece of paper that had the name Mya written on it."

Malik peeked over at her again. "I remember you mentioning that before," he said. "So, Winters is the last name you chose?"

"Not exactly. It's the name that a lady on the staff of the orphanage picked out for me when I was still a baby. When I was ten, I heard one of the other foster kids talking about how their entire name was chosen from someone on staff at the orphanage. It's apparently a common thing."

"Did you ever think about changing your last name to something you want?"

"All the time." There were days that Mya still contemplated changing her last name, but it was a part of her now. "Then I thought about the fact that even if I got my last name from an employee of the orphanage, at least they had a decency to give me a last name, which is more than I can say for my birth parents."

Malik reached over and lightly gripped her hand before placing it back on the steering wheel. "How about we continue the rest of this conversation on the way home?"

"That's a plan," she said with a small grin. "Besides, I need to go over the list that was in the envelope I received."

Mya pulled out her mininotebook that detailed what they needed to discuss with the baker for the wedding. "So, on top of having a cake, Lex and Micah also want a sweets table. The list she gave me is very detailed. She's already talked to the head baker, but she needs me to make sure that the bakery understands everything they want. The right flavors. The right designs."

"And why in the world did they have to pick a bakery so far away?"

Mya laughed. "Lex is a food connoisseur and the bakery we are going to is the best around. They specialize in sweet tables and everything is personalized. And lucky for us, the owner of the bakery was a former Chicago Public Schools student so she is willing to donate sweets for the date auction."

"Very impressive," Malik said to Mya with a smirk.

"How's so?" she asked as she pushed down the automatic button on the door to let some air seep through the crack in the window.

"You just are," he said as he looked at her and held her eyes. *There it was again.* That penetrating stare that made her want to open up even more than she already was.

Mya pulled her eyes away from his and stared out the window just as they were leaving the city and entering the suburbs. If she wasn't careful, she would slowly start letting him in. Although she had to discuss her past with him in order to help with the investigation, she had to try not to cross the thin line between trusting him with information versus trusting him with her heart.

"I can't believe you don't eat sweets," Malik said as they headed back to Chicago.

"That's not true," she said as she slipped off one sandal. "I eat candy every now and then. I'm just not a huge cupcake, brownie, cookie type of girl. There are just some sweets that I like more than others."

"You don't like coffee. You barely eat sweets."

"And I hate working out," she said with a laugh as she lifted a foot to take off her remaining sandal. "All that walking we did has my feet aching." Malik's eyes traveled from the road to her legs. When she reached the strap, she stopped as she followed Malik's gaze.

"I'm sorry, is it okay if I slip off my sandals?" *Is*

it okay? He wanted to tell her she could take off anything she wanted to in his car, but instead, he opted for a head nod in agreement before casting his eyes back to the road.

After she removed her shoes, she curled her feet into the passenger seat and let her arm drape over the open window. The night wind blew her moon-kissed hair over the headrest and she softly closed her eyes as the breeze teased her face. Malik liked seeing Mya so relaxed and he'd enjoyed spending the entire day with her.

After they'd arrived at the bakery, the owner had enthusiastically shared small portions of all the desserts she was going to provide for the date auction. Then she went through a detailed list of all the goodies she was making for Lex and Micah's wedding.

After stuffing their faces with more calories than Malik had ingested in a long time, they had decided to tour the small town before heading back to the city. Neither one of them could have predicted they would have spent an entire day away from work.

"It was nice taking a day off away from everyday responsibilities, wasn't it?" she asked as if reading his mind.

"It really was," Malik agreed. "I haven't taken a day off in so long, I almost forgot what it felt like to spend most of the day not completely focused on my work."

"Neither have I," she said as her eyes remained closed. They drove in comfortable silence for a few more minutes before droplets of rain began to fall. Mya opened her eyes and pulled her hand inside before closing the window.

"I didn't think it was going to rain tonight."

"It wasn't in the city, but I suspect we're going through a rain cloud," Malik said as he turned on his windshield wipers.

"It's coming down pretty hard," Mya said as she leaned closer to the front window before sinking back in her seat. Malik glanced over and noticed she didn't have on a seat belt. He glanced at his dashboard, wondering why it didn't beep.

"Is your seat belt jammed? Maybe you should buckle back up."

"Yes," she said as she pulled the strap and tried to lock the buckle in place. "It jammed like this on me earlier too."

"Damn," Malik muttered under his breath. "When I went to Detroit last weekend, I had my little brother in the car and I think he jammed it. I told that kid not to stick things in the lock."

Mya lifted her head and gave him a curious look. "Umm, I thought all your younger brothers were adults, not kids."

He laughed at her statement. "I meant my little brother from the Big Brothers Big Sisters organization. He's nine and every object that has a hole, he sticks something into."

"I'm part of BBBS too," she said with a smile. "My former little sister is in college now so I figured after I got the after-school program underway, I'd let the organization know I was ready to be assigned another young girl."

Malik returned her smile, not at all surprised that they both were part of the same organization. But by the way Mya was looking at him he assumed she was surprised.

"Are you amazed that you and I happen to have something in common?"

"No, that's not it," she said. "It's just, I didn't grow up with any siblings so being able to be a big sister and make an impact on a young child's life is really rewarding and a feeling I never had before. What about you? How does it compare to the big brother you are for your actual brothers?"

"For me, there's no comparison," Malik said with a laugh. "Although I will always be the oldest, my younger brothers and I aren't that far in age. Micah and I are much closer now than we ever were growing up. While I was into studying and making sure my grades were at the top of the class, Micah was off fooling around in the streets getting into God knows what."

"Ha! Yeah right," Mya retorted. "I've been to your hometown of Cranberry Heights, Arkansas. Didn't exactly strike me as the type of place you could get into much."

"That's not where we grew up," Malik replied. "My parents live there now, but we spent most of our life in Little Rock, Arkansas. Trust me when I say that unlike Cranberry Heights, there is nothing cute and quaint about the area we grew up in."

Malik was used to people assuming that because he graduated from Princeton and was a former profiler for the FBI who was now a private investigator, that he'd lived a cookie-cutter life without many hardships, but that was far from the truth.

"I didn't know that," Mya said softly. "What was it like growing up there?"

"It wasn't always bad," Malik responded. "Back then, we didn't know anything besides Little Rock and with six sons, you can imagine how hard my parents had it sometimes. Believe it or not, one of my fondest memories was that every meal I had always tasted like bacon. That's probably why my brothers and I love bacon so much now."

"Bacon," Mya replied with a look of disbelief. "Am I missing how everything tasting like bacon is a good thing?"

"For us, it was a family bonding moment," he said with a chuckle. "Sometimes we couldn't afford to buy Crisco or cooking oil, so my mom always had to reuse oil we'd used to cook other things. So every day at dinner, we played guess that food."

"Oh wow," Mya said with a laugh. "That's interesting."

"It was," Malik said as he reminisced about his childhood. "And you're looking at the king of the name that food game. Bacon stood no chance against my taste buds."

Mya began laughing hysterically when he pointed to himself and brushed off his shoulders making sure he kept one hand on the wheel as he did so.

"I'm learning quite a few things about your personality that are surprising me," she said when her laughing began to subside.

Malik stopped laughing and glanced from her to the road. "There are still a lot of things you don't know about me, Mya," he said as he increased the speed of his window wipers. *And if I have my way, all of that will be changing sooner than you think.*

Chapter 8

"I bet," Mya said as she turned to the passenger window and masked her smile. She didn't miss the astute look on his face, nor did she miss the meaning behind his statement.

"It's getting pretty bad out there," he stated as he turned on his bright lights to see through the rain. "Any luck with the seat belt?"

Mya had forgotten all about the seat belt and when she tried to lock the buckle again, she still couldn't get it to securely click. "I'm having trouble," she said, wiggling the buckle.

"Let me try," Malik said as he reached over Mya and took the seat belt from her hand. As his arm brushed against her upper thighs in an effort to secure the buckle, Mya tried her best to ignore the sensations she felt.

She watched him look from the road back down to

the buckle, hoping that he didn't notice the rise and fall of her chest had quickened. *Brush it off, Winters*, she thought, giving herself a quick pep talk. She'd already established that Malik had sexy arms. And earlier at the bakery, when they were both sampling one of the desserts, it had taken all her efforts not to focus on the enticing scent of his cologne, but rather the task at hand of tasting the sweet concoction. *I bet his lips taste sweet*, she thought before she could force her brain not to go there.

"Damn it, it's really jammed," he muttered. "See if you can pull a little more slack."

Mya did as she was told, pulling as hard as she could and barely getting any additional slack in the strap. "That's not working."

"I'll try one more time," he said as he pulled the car over to the shoulder of the highway. He used the slack he had to try and force the buckle once more. Mya squeezed her lips together when his hand went even higher up the side of her thigh than it had before. She let out a soft moan when his hand stayed there for a while.

"I'm sorry, did I hurt you?" he asked out of concern.

"Just a little," she told him although it wasn't true. What was she supposed to say? *No, you're not hurting me. I only moaned because having your hands touch my thighs feels good.* Heck no, she couldn't say that!

"I guess I can be heavy-handed sometimes."

"Nope, your hands are perfect," she said breathlessly. *Wait. No.* What did she just say? She hoped it hadn't sounded as seductive out loud as it had in her mind, but a quick glance at Malik proved that it had.

He studied her face for a moment, the only sound between them being the pounding of the rain that was beginning to fall heavier than before.

"You can't say things like that," Malik said as he got back on the road.

"Like what?" Mya asked, pretending not to know what he was referring to.

"You know what," he said, keeping his eyes focused ahead.

"If I knew then I wouldn't be asking," she said, shrugging. Malik shook his head.

"I'll let you get away with playing this game for now, but in the future, I'm making you own up."

She hid another smile. *We'll see about that.* "Own up to what?" she asked innocently. Malik slightly turned his head in her direction when something on the road caught his attention.

"Oh crap," he said as he swerved the SUV around a deer that had dashed across the highway. Mya braced her hands on the dashboard as Malik struggled to regain control of the car.

"Watch out for that other one," Mya yelled when she noticed a smaller deer. The wet roads had her feeling as if they were a puck gliding across an ice rink rather than a car on the highway.

"Brace yourself," Malik said when the car began sliding down a grassy hill. One of Malik's hands was on the wheel while the other was secured across her midsection making sure she didn't get too close to the front window.

Sliding down the hill in the dark seeing nothing but tall grass in the headlights was enough to make her vomit if she hadn't been too busy screaming.

She once heard someone say that their life really had flashed before their eyes when they were in an unfortunate situation. Well, it wasn't exactly her life that was flashing before her, but rather everything she still wanted to accomplish in life before her time came. And out of all the things floating through her mind, the thought of dying before having another chance to kiss Malik by far had to be the craziest thing ever.

Once they cleared the tall grass, the car came to a complete stop, jerking both of their bodies forward when it did.

"Are you okay?" Malik asked as he quickly unbuckled his seat belt and leaned over to her.

"I think so. Do the car lights work?" she asked. She was relieved to find them working when he turned on the interior light but less than thrilled to touch her knee and see blood.

"You're not fine," Malik said as he went in the glove compartment for an alcohol pack and bandage before he reached down to the floor of the backseat and grabbed a water bottle and paper towel. He poured some water on the paper towel and opened the alcohol pack.

"This is going to sting a little," he said softly. Mya was too busy being impressed by the way he was taking immediate care of her to even care that the cut would sting.

"Hssst," she hissed when he touched the cut with the packet. He cleaned up her scratch and then replaced the packet with the refreshing paper towel.

"That should ease the sting."

"It does."

When he moved the paper towel away, he bent over and blew on her cut and placed the bandage on carefully.

"You're really careful with your hands," she said. "You've done this before."

"Once or twice," he said cleaning up the area around her cut. "I worked in the FBI for over eight years before I decided to go into business for myself. Scratches and bruises were a thing of the norm on duty."

"Do you ever miss it?" she asked.

"Sometimes I do," Malik said with a lopsided grin. "But the FBI is nothing like what you see on TV or read in books. Like any job, there are company politics involved and I realized that I'd be more useful if I went into business for myself and used my profiling and investigation skills to help others."

She gave him a soft smile. *Another check mark in Malik's favor*, she thought. The list of cons to dating Malik were becoming slimmer by the second.

"Are you hurt anywhere else?" he asked as he began observing her body.

"No, I'm fine, what about you?"

"I may have a couple bruises, but doesn't feel like anything serious." He pressed the buttons on his GPS. "Looks like the GPS on the car doesn't work so I'll have to check my phone to see if we're near anything."

Mya nodded her head as she picked up her phone and began scrolling through her apps.

"I'm not getting a signal," Malik said.

"Neither am I." Mya was trying not to panic, but

under the current circumstances, she felt like she was allowed to be a little unnerved.

"So, what do we do now?"

"I think I have a map in here," Malik said as he opened the glove compartment. "Here it is."

He began scanning the map. "Here is the last marker I remember seeing," he said as he pointed to a place on the map.

"Um, looks like you're pointing to nothing."

Malik gave her a sideways glance. "When was the last time you looked at a map?"

She shrugged her shoulders. "Why do I need a map when almost every phone and new car has a navigational system installed."

Malik shook his head and laughed. "Maybe so in situations like this, you'll always know where you are."

"I do know where we are," Mya responded. "We're somewhere on the outskirts of Illinois or Wisconsin."

"That's sad," Malik said as he continued to scan the map. "If I weren't here, you wouldn't know which direction to go."

"No, if you weren't here I wouldn't have been out this late in the first place."

"Don't act like you didn't have fun today."

"Well, don't act like I drove the car down a hill because that was definitely you."

Malik looked up from the map. "Did you miss those two deer who went on the road and the heavy rain that's still falling now?"

Mya was about to say something else when Malik interrupted her. "Check this out," he said as he pointed to a place on the map. "Looks like we're right near the grounds of Riviera Ranch Resort and Conference Center."

"I heard that place is gorgeous, but I've never checked it out."

"No time like the present," Malik said as he unlocked his door.

"Ahh, what are you doing?" Mya asked when he touched the door handle.

Malik pointed towards the direction of the field they'd just driven through against their will. "According to this map, if we go up the hill slightly and make a left, there should be a path that will take us directly to the main Riviera Ranch Resort building."

Mya glanced around into the darkness. "I'm not going out into a field at night because of that little spot on the map."

Malik lifted an eyebrow at her. "Unless you want to stay in this car overnight, we have to go somewhere to at least get phone service. No one knows we're out here."

"That's not true," Mya replied. "Lex and Micah know we had to go to the bakery today."

"Did they know you and I were going together?" Malik asked.

"I told Lex you were coming with me."

"And I told Micah the same thing, so what makes you think they wouldn't just assume we decided not to come back to Chicago until tomorrow."

"Come on," Mya said. "They wouldn't assume…" Her words trailed off as she thought about her friends who were probably all cozied up with their significant others.

"You're right, we're screwed if we stay here."

Malik laughed. "That's the most agreeable you've been with me since we met."

"Not true."

"Yes it is."

"No it's not."

"Mya," Malik said as he reached for the door handle again.

"Sorry," she replied as she slipped her sandals back on. "I think the accident has me a little jumpy."

"I know," Malik said with a warm smile. "I'll get the large umbrella out of the trunk and we'll begin making our way in the direction of the ranch."

As Malik got out of the car to retrieve the umbrella, Mya took a moment to lean her head against the headrest. It was hard enough to spend the entire day with Malik and keep her hormones in check, let alone spend the entire night with him as well. They needed to find shelter and fast because there was no way she was spending the night cooped up in the fields with a man who was testing her ability to keep her hands to herself.

Just focus on walking straight ahead, Malik thought as they followed a path that he hoped would take them to Riviera Ranch and Resort.

He tried to concentrate on protecting Mya. But when she jumped closer to him with every sound she heard, it became more difficult to keep his hands on the stem of the umbrella rather than pull her to him.

"What's that?" she asked as she clutched his arm tighter.

"It's probably just a farm animal of some sort. I think we're close to the main resort building."

It was hard to see past all the tall grass, but Malik knew that a path this well kept meant they were close to some type of civilization. He still couldn't believe that he'd lost control of the car, but the most important thing was that they were both okay and he'd managed to avoid hitting the deer. No doubt the accident could have been worse had that happened.

"What are you going to do about your car?" Mya asked.

"Once we get someplace safe, I'll call my insurance company and let them know what happened. But the damage wasn't too bad, so a tow truck should be able to pull it up the hill and back onto the road. "

"Sounds good," she said through chattered teeth.

"Are you cold?"

"Only because of the rain. This sweater I brought is a little thin for this weather."

"Here you go," Malik said taking off his jacket. "This should help and it's water resistant."

"Thank you," Mya said uncurling her arm from his to put on the jacket.

"Man," Malik said when she zipped it closed. "It swallows you." His jacket fell at her knees and was actually a little longer than her dress.

"I love that it swallows me," she said with a smile. "Less places for water to touch me, especially since we don't know how much further we have to walk."

"Not that much further," Malik said as a large well-lit building came into view. "Check that out over there." He pointed in the direction of the building.

"Thank goodness," Mya said linking her arm back in his. "Good decision, Malik. You were right."

Malik stopped walking forcing Mya to stop as well. "I'm sorry, what did you just say?"

She turned an eyebrow up at him. "I'm not repeating it, so you might as well just soak in that moment."

"You don't have to say it again," he said as they continued walking. "You said I was right. Did you hear that, people?" he shouted. "Mya Winters admitted that I, Malik Madden, was right."

"Oh my God did you really have to scream that out loud. We don't know what's out here."

"Rare moments cause for rare behavior," he said just as they were approaching the building.

"Whatever," she said with a laugh. "I never thought I'd be so excited to see a building in my entire life. I thought we were going to have to sleep in the car."

"Me too," Malik said as he opened the door to the Riviera Ranch Resort and Conference Center. "I had already planned a pep talk to make you feel as if we were just camping in a car rather than stuck out in a field."

"That would have been sweet of you." Mya grinned up at him as she went through the door. "But I still would have been scared."

He returned her grin before soaking in the lodge like atmosphere of the lobby. "This place is nice," he said as he glanced around for an attendant since no one was at the front desk.

"This ranch has been in the Riviera family for years and now, it's owned by Alvero Riviera II. Although it's also a convention center, it has a really intimate feel...nothing like it in the area. This place is known for it's rustic elegance and decor with Cuban flare. Hundreds of events take place here year-round no matter what the season and any time we try to plan events here, we know we have to book at least six months to a year or more in advance. Imani and Cyd have been here quite a few times, but every time we have an event here, I'm too busy planning another event the same day."

"I can see why people love this place," Malik said as he observed the craftsmanship of the furniture. "I wonder if these are all customized furniture pieces or if they are store-bought. Something tells me this is the type of place that gets customized pieces."

"You're right about that," said a gentleman who Malik and Mya hadn't heard approach them from behind. "Every piece of furniture in our main lobby is customized."

Malik and Mya turned to greet the man that appeared. "I'm Alvero Riviera III, but everyone calls me Vero. Welcome to our family ranch resort and convention center."

"It's a pleasure to meet you, Vero," Malik said, accepting his handshake. "I'm Malik Madden and this is my friend Mya Winters. Our car went off the road about a mile away and we were hoping you still had rooms available."

"You're in luck," Vero said as he walked over to the front desk. "There are a few guests on the grounds tonight who came early for a conference, and tomorrow other guests will start to arrive midmorning or early afternoon. An hour before our desk clerk left, I believe she said we had at least three rooms still available. Let me see what I can do for you."

"Thanks, Vero," Mya said. "I'm one of the cofounders of Elite Events and I've heard great things about your ranch resort."

"Oh, yes," he said with excitement. "I've worked with Imani and Cydney before. So nice to meet another member of Elite Events."

"Likewise," Mya said with a smile as she shook his hand.

"Okay," Vero said as he entered a few more keys into the keyboard. "Your room will be located on the third floor in the east wing."

Malik glanced over at Mya before turning back to Vero. "Are both rooms on the third floor in the east wing?"

"Nope, just the one," Vero said, punching in a few more keys. "Our desk clerk must have reserved the other two for guests before she went home for the night. There's only one room, so you'll have to share."

Chapter 9

Share a room? Mya shook her head assuming she'd heard him incorrectly. "Did you just say we have to share a room?" she asked Vero.

"Yes, ma'am. We only have one room available tonight."

Mya looked up at the ceiling and sighed. She wasn't the type to put much faith into zodiac signs, but when she'd been standing in line at a café yesterday scrolling through her Facebook newsfeed, she had come across an article on horoscopes. The article had told her that this week she should expect the unexpected. Glancing over at Malik, she realized that ever since they had begun spending time together, expecting the unexpected had seemed to be their norm.

"Oh, wait," Vero said. "I read that wrong. We do have two rooms available, but they are connected. Would you like to reserve those two rooms instead?"

"Yes," Mya answered almost immediately, which gained a laugh from Malik. "We'll take those."

"Excellent. The location is still on the third floor in the east wing." They placed their credit cards on file and received their room keys from Vero.

"Here's a map as well," Vero said as he handed them each a packet. "Tomorrow morning, our complimentary hot breakfast is from 6:00 a.m. to 9:00 a.m. in the back of the lobby. My father and other family members greet the guests and answer any questions you may have about the history of the Riviera Ranch Resort and Conference Center during that time. We also have a few activities listed in the packet."

"Thank you," Malik said as he accepted the booklet. "Will there be someone in the lobby for me to talk to about my car? I'm calling my insurance company as well."

"Yes, someone will definitely be able to help you. If no one can, they will call me and I can help."

"I appreciate it," Malik said before turning to Mya. "Ready to head to our rooms?" he asked.

"Sure am," she responded as they bid Vero goodnight. Even though she wasn't sharing a room with Malik, she couldn't help but think about what would have happened if they had been forced to share a room together. Neither one of them had an extra change of clothes, so she would have had to either sleep in her wet dress or sleep in her bra and panties. When they arrived to their rooms, she was glad she didn't have to make that decision.

"Hope you sleep well," Malik said standing in the hallway as he opened the door to his room.

"You too," Mya said as she entered her room and

shut the door. "Man, this was a long day," she said to herself as she briefly admired the room on her way to the bathroom. When she looked at herself in the mirror, she cringed at the image staring back at her.

Not only was she still pretty damp from the rain, but the curls in her hair had fallen and her skin was flushed. After walking a mile in the rain she should be glad that the damage wasn't worse. She reached behind her and tugged at the zipper of her dress.

"Come on," she said aloud as she tugged at the zipper again. She glanced at her reflection once more and scanned the bathroom to see what cosmetics they provided. Luckily the resort gave the guests a toothbrush and toothpaste in addition to the other basic amenities that most resorts had in the rooms.

Thank goodness I packed that extra pair of panties, Mya thought to herself, although she didn't know why she was even stressing out about how she would look tomorrow when there wasn't much she could do at this point. Whenever she was traveling to a place that was more than an hour away, Mya had a habit of packing a pair of underwear just in case something like this happened.

Now all she had to do before she hopped in the shower was get her dress off, wash it in the sink, and hope that it was dry by the morning or else she would have to dry it with the blow-dryer.

After her tenth tug, she realized that the dress wasn't coming off without some help. She sighed before walking over to the connecting doors, surprised to see both doors were cracked open.

"Malik, are you here?" she called out into his room.

"Yes, I'm here," he said.

"Great, I need your help and I noticed that the doors were still open," she said pushing her way through them.

"I noticed it too," Malik replied. "But I didn't want to close the door in case you needed me. I figured I'd let you decide if you wanted the doors completely shut."

"That's nice of you," she said as she got closer to the bathroom. "But I think…" Her words trailed off when she finally reached his bathroom. He stood near the granite sink sporting nothing more than a white towel. And she was caught off guard by the sexiest body she'd ever seen.

"I'll be okay," she finally said finishing her sentence. When he turned to her, she didn't even try to stop her eyes from studying every muscle and ab on his honey-brown body or the perfect V shape of his torso that disappeared under the fabric hanging off his waist.

"Did you need me for anything?" Malik asked with a sly smile on his face.

"Probably not what you think I need you for," Mya replied as she walked into the bathroom putting on a confident facade.

"Well your eyes were just singing a different tune a few moments ago."

"Yeah well, now all of me is on the same tune. I need you to help me take my dress off."

When the fire in his eyes began to build, she tried to cover up the choice of words she'd used. "I meant, my zipper is stuck and I need your help unzipping it."

"Are you sure that's all you need help with?" Malik asked as he motioned for her to turn around so he could help her. She obeyed and turned around, anxious to avoid direct eye contact with him.

"I'm sure," she said self-assuredly. But when his hands began to work the zipper, lightly grazing her skin as he did so, confident was the last thing she felt.

"It's pretty jammed," he said as his hand moved inside the top of her dress to try and work the zipper from another angle. She could feel the heat from his body on her back teasing her senses and causing her to react in ways she had to fight hard to control.

"I think I have it," he said as he wiggled the zipper once more until it finally gave. As his hands slid the zipper down her back, she found herself holding her breath. When he reached the back of her bra, she felt his hands slow down stopping right underneath the clasp before he placed a featherlike touch on the middle of her back.

"Um, I think you're good now," he said as he cleared his throat. Only then did Mya release her breath and turn around to face him, making sure to hold up her dress so it didn't fall to the floor. *Oh lord.* They were standing much closer than she had originally thought they were, and his chest and abs were in her direct line of vision. Her eyes took the opportunity to scan him even closer.

Mya had never been too affected by a man with a nice body. She'd always known that it wasn't just about how a man looked. It was about his mind as well. She had to be attracted to both to even allow herself to get carried away with a man.

From the way she admired Malik, she was very aware that her body realized he was a man with a godlike physique and a sexy mind. Triple threat if you considered the fact that he had accomplished a lot in his career and was also a man who knew what he wanted.

She gazed up at him trying to think of one good reason why she should turn around and walk out of the room before she did something crazy like lean in closer to him in hopes that he would kiss her.

What are you thinking? she asked herself as she closed her eyes in a long blink. *Don't just stand there with your dress falling off. Go back to your room.* Her heart and body were disagreeing with the thoughts floating around in her mind. But she decided to listen to her head and walk back to her room.

She took one step back, only for Malik to take one step forward. Her breath caught in her throat again. She took another step back to help her along, and then another so that she was now standing right outside the bathroom.

"If you're trying to go back to your room to hide out, I suggest you do it a lot quicker," he said in a raspy voice. It was obvious that he was feeling the exact same emotions as she was. She knew if she didn't heed to his warning, they may go further than she was prepared for them to go in that moment.

But she couldn't get her feet to step backwards any more, especially after he looked at her like she was a decadent dessert after a three-course meal. His eyes were blazing with desire. A flame she knew she had lit by coming into his room.

"Mya," he said as he took a couple steps toward her. "Unless you're ready for me to kiss you, I suggest you go back to your room before I lose my patience."

She studied his features watching his body tense

up before her eyes. He was struggling to maintain his composure as the sexual tension continued to rise the longer she stayed.

He stepped to her again, so close that it wouldn't take much for her to reach out and pull him to her. Her eyes dropped down to his mouth.

"When you look at me like that," he said as he began bringing his mouth towards hers, "you make it hard for me to deny myself a taste."

"Then don't," she heard herself say, causing him to stop right before his lips touched hers. He searched her eyes and instead of kissing her, he moved to her neck, placing a soft kiss right behind her ear. His tongue swirled small circles on her sweet spot until Mya released a soft moan. The teasing was over as quickly as it started.

Malik snaked one arm behind her back and pulled her into his embrace. At the same time, his other hand went behind her head. Slowly, he brought his lips down on hers in such a seductive way that Mya had barely processed what was coming next before it happened.

She felt his kiss travel all the way to her toes, feeding her desire even more. Just as she'd predicted, lips like his were made for kissing. The gentle methodical movements of his tongue reached parts of her that no man had ever even come close to reaching before.

Forgotten was the fact that she was supposed to be holding up her dress. And instead of caring that the material was now lying on the floor, she cared more about her wish for his towel to join her dress.

As hands explored bodies and his lips became well acquainted with parts other than her mouth, Mya realized that it would be hard for a person nearby to tell whether or not they were kissing or having sex.

When his groan sent a chill throughout her entire body, she broke their kiss by stepping back from the arms that had made her a willing hostage.

Mya watched Malik fight to regain control, the result of his desire straining against the white towel that she'd bet wouldn't remain tied at his waist for much longer.

"I should go back to my room now," she said as she picked up her dress, not bothering to cover up her bra and panties.

"I think that's a good idea," Malik said as he ran his fingers over his face before lifting his head to the ceiling.

Mya was almost to the connecting doors when he called out to her. She stopped and looked over her left shoulder and caught him admiring her cheeky white-and-teal panties with the words *If You Dare* stamped across them.

He chuckled as he shook his head. "Nice," he said as he pointed to her panties.

"Thanks," she said with a slight smile.

He brought his eyes back to her face. "I figure you'll keep your side of the connecting doors locked and closed, which is fine. But I will leave my side cracked."

He held her gaze as if to make sure she got his message. She had received the message loud and clear.

"Okay," she said as she scattered and headed straight to the bathroom to finally take a much needed shower.

Two hours later, after she was showered and lying

in between the plush white comforter and sheets, she was still having trouble falling asleep.

"Damn you, Malik Madden," she muttered under her breath in sexual frustration as she punched her fists into the covers. She grabbed her phone, tapped on her Pandora app and closed her eyes as she listened to the soft R&B music in hopes that she'd finally fall asleep. *If I'm lucky, I'll have a dream or two about the man in the room next door,* she thought as she drifted to sleep.

Chapter 10

After Malik got his food from the hot breakfast buffet, he went to the beverage station to pour a much-needed cup of coffee. He had barely got an hour worth of sleep last night, and had finally decided at 5am to face the inevitable. There would be no sleeping as long as Mya Winters was in the room next door.

He'd already spoken to his insurance company and worked with Vero who was nice enough to have a tow truck pull him out of the grassy ditch he'd fallen into last night.

He'd had the front desk call Mya's room so they could eat breakfast and get on the road right away. He wasn't so much anxious to get back to Chicago, but he did have a few meetings this afternoon. And after barely getting any sleep, he had to try and take a nap beforehand.

There were a few people scattered around the lobby having breakfast, but for the most part, he hadn't seen that many guests since most of the conference folks were due to arrive later. He had his choice of great seating, but he chose to sit at the table with the amazing view of the Riviera Ranch Resort and Conference Center property.

"This is so good," he said while tasting his coffee and savoring the sip.

"That's because it's imported directly from this great coffee farm in Cuba," said a boisterous, friendly man who looked like an older version of Vero.

"You must be Alvero Riviera II," Malik said as he stood to shake the man's outreached hand.

"That I am," he said with a hearty laugh. "But everyone calls me Al."

"Nice to meet you, Al," Malik replied. "Would you like to take a seat? I have a friend who would enjoy meeting you. She's an event planner and she loves your ranch resort."

"Well, don't mind if I do," Al said. "Any lover of our property is someone I have to meet."

For the first time, Malik noticed the white cane Al was holding. Al felt around the table until he found the seat and sat down.

"My son Vero was telling me about you earlier this morning," Al said. "Did he help you with your car?"

"He sure did," Malik responded. "Luckily, there wasn't much damage and between what I knew about cars and what your son knows, my SUV is running well enough to get us home. This place is only an hour away from the city anyway, so I'm confident we'll be fine."

"That's good to hear," Al said. "I hope you enjoyed your stay here. Maybe next time you'll stay for a bit longer."

Malik was about to respond to Al, when Mya walked into the lobby area, her brown waves bouncing around her shoulders. She didn't look at all like they'd driven in a ditch last night and gotten caught in the rain, nor did she look like she had as restless of a night as he had.

When she got closer to the table, Malik also noticed how fresh and clean her face looked. She wasn't one of those women who wore a lot of makeup, but seeing her face free of it made him all hot and bothered in places that he couldn't afford to be hot and bothered in right now.

"Hello, gentlemen," Mya said as she approached the table. She gave Malik a soft smile before turning to Al.

"Hello, sir, I'm Mya Winters." She extended her hand.

"Hi, Mya," Al said as he reached out his hand to feel for hers. "I've always loved the name Mya."

Malik watched Mya's eyes follow the wavering of Al's hand and catching on quickly, she immediately reached out and clasped her hand over Al's. "It's a pleasure to meet you," Al continued. "I'm Alvero Riviera II, but everyone calls me Al. Your friend Malik here was just telling me how much you like the property."

"I do," Mya said with excitement. "I'm one of the co-owners of Elite Events Inc. and my partners, Imani and Cyd, always gush over how great the events turn out that we plan here."

"Oh, yes," Al said. "I know Elite Events. It's always nice to hear event planners talk about our ranch resort so positively. As I told Malik, next time, you should make your stay longer."

Malik turned back to face Al. "I'm sorry, yes of course we will definitely stay longer next time."

"I'll be right back," Mya said pointing to the breakfast buffet. "I'm going to grab a bagel and some fruit."

As she walked away, Malik stole a glance in her direction, enjoying the fact that he couldn't get caught staring.

"You know," Al said interrupting his observation of Mya. "Just because I'm blind doesn't mean I can't tell when a man and a woman are attracted to one another."

Malik laughed. "Naw, we're just friends."

"Right," Al said. "And I'm not really blind, I just wear these sunglasses and use this cane as a fashion statement."

Malik laughed a little louder this time. "Well, I may be attracted to her, but she isn't ready to date a man like me."

"And why is that?" Al asked.

Malik glanced back over to Mya who was now at the beverage station. "I'm the best man and she's the maid of honor for our friends' wedding. Plus, I'm helping her with a huge event and you know what they say about mixing business with pleasure."

"I've always disagreed with that saying," Al replied. "Sometimes, we can't help who we fall for any more than we can stop ourselves from falling."

"Timing is everything," Malik said as he took a

sip of his coffee. "I'm trying to wait for the right time to tell her how I feel."

"Ahh, I see," Al said. "This isn't about timing being perfect for her. It's about timing being perfect for you. There's something that you're afraid to tell her."

Malik sat upright in his chair, surprised Al had picked up on something he had never voiced. "I just meant timing in general," Malik responded.

"Take it from a old man who just told his oldest son the same thing," Al said as he lifted a finger into the air. "Time waits for no one. While you're sitting around trying to figure out how to tell her whatever it is you don't want her to know, the harder it will be for her to hear what it is you have to say."

Malik let Al's words sink in. "That's the same thing that my father always tells me."

"Us old men tend to talk from experience," Al said with a laugh. "My wife and I have always agreed to be honest with our children so that they could learn from our mistakes."

Malik sighed as he thought about the things he wanted to tell Mya, but wasn't sure he could just yet.

"We can't ask a woman to be open and honest with us if we aren't willing to do the same," Al added. "Mya's a good woman. I can tell a lot about a person within the first few minutes of meeting them. Trust her with your thoughts and the reward will be more than you could have ever dreamed of."

Malik stared at Al and shook his head. "I'm great at reading people, but people are often terrible at reading me."

"Son, I wasn't born blind," Al said. "But when I

lost my sight, my other senses became stronger than ever. I can't judge a first impression off a look or a statement because I can't see how a person looks as they speak or pick up on those social cues. So I trained myself to pick up on what's in here," he said pointing to his heart.

"Seems like I missed some great conversation," Mya said as she approached and sat beside Malik.

"You're right on time," Al replied. "Malik was just about to tell me about this event you two are planning."

Mya's eyes lit up the same way they did every time she talked about the date auction. "In order to raise money to fund an after-school program in Chicago, Elite Events with the help of our sponsors, including Malik, are hosting a date auction next weekend."

"Smart and cares for the community," Al said. "Malik, don't let her slip away."

Both Malik and Mya laughed at Al's comment. "Thanks, Al," Mya said. "Everything will be perfect as soon as we lock in a venue."

"You don't have a venue even though it's next weekend?"

"Our venue fell through and there is so much going on in Chicago that all the really great places are taken. We need a place to accommodate at least 500 possible attendees. The event is nine days away so we may have to get more creative and do something outside and pray the weather cooperates."

"I'm sorry to hear that," Al said as he took out his cell phone. "Hi, Vero, didn't you say that you received a call from the McHenrys?"

Malik glanced at Mya who lifted her shoulders

to imply that she wasn't sure why Al had suddenly decided to call his son. After a few *I see*s as their conversation switched from English to Spanish, Al ended the call.

"Can you think of anything more unfortunate than surprising your fiancé with a trip to Vegas and having him run off with a Kim Kardasian look-alike?"

"Um, not really," Mya said with a laugh. Malik followed suit.

"Well luckily for the two of you, the Kardasians just saved you the hassle of having your event outside with this unpredictable Chicago weather."

"Please say you mean what I think you mean," Mya said with excitement.

"I'd say that someone is definitely looking out for the two of you because we're booked through the rest of the year, but next weekend just opened up. Do you want the slot?"

"Absolutely," Mya squealed.

"Thanks for making this happen, Al," Malik added.

"We enjoy doing events for a good cause and we'll donate as well. Once you finish eating, come find me and we'll take you on a tour of the grounds."

"We will," Malik said when Al stood up.

"And think about what I said, Malik," Al said as he walked away.

"What does he want you to think about?" Mya asked.

"Nothing," Malik said turning his attention back to Mya who was about to take a bite of her bagel. "See, aren't you glad the car slid down that grassy hill so close to Riviera Ranch Resort and Conference Center?"

Mya stopped her hand before the bagel reached her mouth. "You're right, Malik. Next time a venue cancels on us, I'll be sure to give you a call so we can almost hit two deer, drive down a grassy hill in the middle of a thunderstorm and get stuck an hour away from the city without a change of clothes." She laughed before she finally took a bite.

Malik smiled, glad to see his feisty Mya was back to snap him out of the sappy way his talk with Al had left him feeling.

On the drive home, Malik asked Mya a few more questions about the call she'd received and Mya agreed to hand over her work cell for a few hours later in the week. Once he stated that he had enough information to start the investigation, they drove in silence for most of the ride home.

Now, they were only thirty minutes away from her place and for some odd reason, Mya became interested in Malik answering a few questions of her own.

"So," she said as she stretched out her arms before placing her hands back in her lap. "What was it like growing up in a large family?"

Malik peeked over at her and flashed her a big smile. "There was always someone to talk to and hang out with, but that also meant there was always someone in your business."

"I can imagine," she said as she thought about six boys running around under the same roof.

"At one point, both my parents lost their jobs so me, Micah and Malakai did anything we could to bring in extra money to help take care of the triplets, Crayson, Caden and Carter."

As Malik continued to talk about his childhood, Mya listened intently at the way he described his siblings. The love and bond they shared was something she wished she'd experienced growing up.

"By the way you talk about your neighborhood in Little Rock, it seems like it was a hard place for a young man to grow up without getting involved with anything illegal."

"It was," Malik said as his face grew more serious. "There were a lot of things we didn't talk about growing up. My parents had a strict rule about all their boys going to school and getting good grades. But I was always perceptive, so I knew which of my brothers were truly doing what they said they were doing. And also, which of my brothers like Micah, had been saying one thing and doing another. My parents raised some smart men and whether we used our smarts back then for educational or street purposes, the most important thing is that we're all using our skills for good today."

"That's good to hear," Mya said. "Hearing you talk reminds me why I fight so hard for the Chicago after-school programs."

"Kids need someone willing to fight for them," Malik said. "Before moving to Cranberry Heights, my dad was a community director and my mom was a teacher. They both dedicated their lives for helping students."

"Now I see where you get it from," Mya said with a smile. "You're right, kids do need someone willing to fight for them. I remember every teacher or community leader I ever met who offered me a piece of advice that changed my life."

Mya thought back to when she was a teenager. It had been one of the hardest times in her life. "When I was sixteen, I witnessed one of the girls in the foster home I was in at the time get slapped across the face several times by the woman of the household because she had snuck an extra slice of bread. The girl had always treated me poorly and on more than one occasion, she had taken my food off my plate knowing that I couldn't tell anybody because somehow, I would be the one to blame. I remember helping the girl wash her face and her apologizing profusely for stealing my food and that she didn't know why she was so hungry."

Mya adjusted herself in her seat. "The next day, I got home from school and the woman was waiting for me with a belt in her hand. Turns out the girl told her that I was the one stealing the food. I remember the woman hitting me across my back for about ten strokes and with each stroke, I made a vow that I would never allow anyone else to lay their hands on me again."

"I'm sorry that happened to you," Malik said as he leaned over and squeezed her hand the same way he had yesterday. *I could really get used to this type of comfort*, she thought.

"What did you do after that? Did you approach the girl or tell the woman you didn't do it?"

"Nope," Mya said shaking her head. "I'd already told the woman I didn't do it and there was no point talking to the girl. Quite frankly, I think she wanted an excuse to use her belt on me. I'd been in two homes before that one and each foster home had a different set of rules and punishments. I went upstairs and washed up for dinner just like I would have any other day and then, in the middle of the night, I snuck out while everyone was sleeping."

"That was really brave of you. Making that decision had to be tough," Malik said, his right hand still over hers.

"It was," she replied as she glanced out the window. "I know there are a lot of good foster parents out there, but my experiences weren't all milk and cookies. Walking out of that foster home was the best decision I ever made and it was the foundation for my inner strength. I realized then that in order to succeed and build a better life for myself, I had to hold all the cards to my future in my hands."

Chapter 11

Malik stood back and watched Mya in awe as she worked the room during their informational date-auction meet and greet that was being held at a downtown hotel.

Within days of them returning to Chicago, two news anchors mentioned the date auction on local stations and Mya had given several interviews about the auction as well. Calls from local celebrities and community members came flooding in from people who not only wanted to donate money, but were also interested in being auctioned off. Elite Events also received a variety of gift certificates from restaurants, bars, hotels, activity centers and organizations willing to sponsor dates for the lucky couples.

On Saturday, they released the secret location of the date auction to give attendees a week to make travel plans and were rewarded by even more people on the outskirts of Chicago interested in attending the date auction. The preregistrations were rolling in and they were definitely on-target to meet the mark of five hundred attendees and possibly exceed it.

Now, with four days left until the auction, they had decided to extend to twenty-five date-auction candidates instead of the original twenty. The event would also feature live musical entertainment and raffles throughout the day for lucky singles in the audience.

Malik was amazed at the outpouring of support they received, but he was even more impressed by the woman who was making it all happen.

"Have you asked her out on a date yet?"

Malik turned to find his cousin, Winter Dupree, approaching him. "No, I haven't. I was waiting until after the date auction to officially ask her out."

Winter gave him a look of disbelief. "Um, I hate to state the obvious but have you seen how much male attention she's been getting tonight."

Malik crossed his arms over his chest as he continued to observe Mya. "Yeah, I noticed."

"And," Winter said waving her hands in a motion for him to continue.

"And, I've decided to wait until after the auction," he repeated.

"You know, for someone with such a high IQ and your trained skills, you often lack in opportunities to seize the moment."

"So you've pointed out on more than one occasion."

"And I'll keep pointing it out until you decide to listen." Winter stood in front of him to block his view of Mya. "Look, Malik, you didn't decide to spend all this time in Chicago to watch Mya from a distance.

If I felt like she wasn't interested, I'd tell you not to bother." Winter glanced over her shoulder at Mya. "But she's been watching you tonight just as hard as you're watching her and I know I'm not the only person here who is picking up on the signs. How about you grow some balls and just ask her out tonight. She probably needs a break before the chaos of the auction."

Malik waited for her to move back to his side, but she didn't. "Okay, I'll think about it," he finally said.

"I guess that's better than a no," Winter said before she walked away. It wasn't that Malik didn't want to ask her out. They'd had dinner together on two other occasions during the past five days, but both times had been to talk about the date auction. But yesterday, Malik had gotten some information regarding her investigation and he didn't want Mya to be too concerned with his findings so close to the auction.

That's not playing by the rules, Malik thought. *You're her private investigator first and friend second.* Under any other circumstance, he wouldn't hesitate to divulge the information he'd found. Much like him, Mya kept certain parts of herself guarded from those who might pass judgment without getting to know her first. He knew a large part of why she had opened up to him was because she had needed his services to hopefully find some answers about her past. He'd spent more time with Mya this past month than he'd remembered spending time with anyone else outside of members of his family, which said a lot about his relationships with women from his past.

In the middle of her conversation with a few date-auction candidates, she glanced over at him and caught his eye. He wished so many people weren't surrounding them, but he enjoyed seeing her in her element. Malik was quickly learning that people were drawn to Mya and while he liked seeing her network the room, what he enjoyed even more was the way she held his gaze in the midst of conversations with others.

When a few people dispersed, leaving her alone for the first time tonight, he walked over toward her.

"You did a great job tonight," Malik said when he made it to her. "And you look amazing," he added as he admired her outfit. She looked beautiful in her navy blue dress that hit just above the knee and matching navy blue pumps.

"Thanks, Malik," she said as she tilted her head to the side and smiled. "You don't look too bad yourself." She touched the collar of his crème summer blazer before lifting her almond shaped eyes to him.

"Everything is definitely falling into place."

"It really is," she said glancing around the room. "And I hate to admit it, but having your help wasn't that bad."

Malik placed his hand over his heart and flashed his pearly whites. "Do you think you can repeat those words so everyone in the room can hear you?" he asked loudly.

"See, I was trying to be nice to you, but you just couldn't help yourself," she said pointing a finger at him.

"Okay, okay," he said putting his hands up in defeat. "Thanks for the compliment."

She squinted her eyes at him before responding. "You're welcome."

He leaned in closer to her ear. "You don't have to tell everyone that you enjoy being around me. I'll settle for you showing your appreciation in a place more private."

She gasped and although the noise was faint, he still managed to hear it. He looked back at her face and forced his gaze to remain on her eyes and not her lips.

"Great session," said a male voice, interrupting their conversation, or current lack thereof. Mya and Malik both greeted one of the candidates for the date auction.

"Mya, I can tell you care so much about this cause. That's very admirable."

He must not see me standing here, Malik thought, suddenly feeling very possessive.

"Thank you," Mya said glancing from Malik to the man.

"You're welcome. You really look beautiful tonight." His eyes raked over her.

"Why thanks," she said flipping her hair over her shoulder. But Malik knew the act wasn't a flirtatious one. There was a certain way Mya flipped her hair when she was flirting and a certain way she flipped her hair when she didn't really want to be bothered, but had to remain sociable. This hair flip was definitely the latter.

Evidently, the man couldn't tell the difference since he continued to give her compliments and maintain conversation.

"Everyone seems to be leaving," Malik said as he nodded his head to the exit door. "The session is over so we'll be in touch with everyone Thursday or Friday if we have any additional information."

Malik was losing his patience with the candidate. Mya wasn't interested and he wasn't just thinking that because he was interested in her. Her body language said it all.

"I'll leave in a minute," the guy said to Malik.

"No," Malik said stepping closer to Mya and wrapping a possessive arm around her waist. "I think you should be leaving now."

He felt Mya's eyes on him. She was a firecracker and there was no doubt in his mind that she would put him in his place if she felt like he'd overstepped. When Mya didn't say anything to his statement, he pulled her even closer.

The guy looked from Mya to Malik before setting his eyes back on Mya. "I guess I'll be leaving now," he said to Mya. "Maybe after the auction we can meet up to discuss the after-school program. It's refreshing to find a woman passionate about something other than motherhood or household issues. You know, real life concerns."

Dumb ass, Malik thought after the man made his last comment.

"Excuse me for a second, Malik," Mya said as she stepped out of his wrapped arm.

"I must have heard you wrong," Mya said getting closer to the man. "Because your last comment really made you sound like an egotistical jerk."

"You know what I meant," he retaliated.

"I'm not sure I do," Mya said crossing her arms over her chest. She glanced around the room. "Listen, I don't want to embarrass you in front of the remain-

ing women in the room, so how about you excuse
yourself like Malik asked you to do."

The man looked from Mya to Malik again before
finally walking away.

"Can we get out of here and head to a late-night
café or something?" Malik asked after most of the
attendees had exited.

"I have a better idea," Mya said as she picked up
her purse. "My place is only a few blocks away. Are
you interested in a nightcap?"

Malik studied her expression, a little surprised
she'd invited him to her place. He'd assumed they'd
been meeting at public places ever since that explo-
sive kiss at Riviera Ranch Resort and Conference
Center to avoid being alone with one another again.
He was fine with letting her control the places they
met until after the auction was over, and he didn't assume that something physical would happen if they
went to her place. But the sexual tension was even
stronger since they had kissed and if Mya wanted to
end the night at her place, he wouldn't be the one to
stop it.

"I'll follow you in my car."

Mya lit a few candles, took out two wineglasses,
and ran her fingers through her hair to get rid of any
unruly stands. After they'd arrived at her place and
Mya had shown Malik where to park, he'd insisted
on stopping in the liquor store on the corner to pick
up some wine.

Mya didn't have a clue what was going to happen
tonight, but she knew that whatever the night had in
store, she wasn't backing down. There was only so

much sexual frustration a woman could take. And after Malik had gotten all possessive of her after their informational date-auction session, it had taken all her energy not to pull him in for a kiss in front of everyone in that room.

She was so wrapped up in her own thoughts that she jumped at the sound of the buzzer. After confirming it was Malik and buzzing him up, she stood in the doorway and awaited his arrival.

The minute he stepped off the elevator, she felt her stomach drop. He had the same look in his eyes that she knew was reflected in hers.

"Thanks for picking up the wine," she said as she let him in and shut the door.

"You're welcome," he replied removing his blazer and handing it to her. "Your place looks really nice." He moved into the living room.

"Thanks. How about I give you a quick tour." *Emphasis on the quick part.* It wasn't that she was ready to jump in bed with him now that he was in her home. But making out never hurt anyone and she was definitely ready to taste his perfect lips again.

When they made it back to the living room, they settled on her couch. Mya observed Malik while he poured the wine, taking note that something seemed to be slightly different with him than moments earlier.

"Is everything okay?" she asked when he passed her a wineglass. He gave her a guarded look.

"Everything is fine," he said taking a sip.

"I call BS," she said taking a sip of the wine as well. "What is it?"

He studied her eyes. "I was really debating on whether or not I wanted to bring this up to you tonight. But considering you told me to notify you the minute I found out anything solid about your case, I owe it to you to tell you what I know."

Mya's heart began beating a mile a minute as she let his words sink in. *He has answers about my past.* Granted, this wasn't exactly the most ideal timing, but he was right, she wanted to know.

"What is it?" she asked.

"I found out where the call you received came from," he said as he placed his wineglass on the table. "It came from the Senior Suites of Central Station about a mile away from me."

Mya gasped as her hand flew to her mouth. "The call came from Senior Suites? Ms. Bee lives there. After I ran away from that terrible foster home, I ended up in a women and child shelter in the city. Ms. Bee volunteered there at the time and we connected in a way I hadn't with any other adult. She took me in until I graduated from high school."

"That would explain why I found your name on a few of her senior living documents."

"Yes, she loves it there. Since she never had any children of her own, I became her family. I set up her living quarters and I'm also her point of contact for emergencies or any decisions that need additional input. The folks that reside there have become really close friends to her." She took a sip of her wine. "Are you sure the call came from there? It didn't sound like Ms. Bee's voice."

"I'm positive," Malik stated. "But that doesn't mean it was Ms. Bee who called."

"That's true. I'd planned on stopping by to see her

tomorrow. I go by there the same time every other week or so."

Malik gently touched her hand. "Would you like me to go with you?" he asked. Mya really didn't have to think hard about her answer.

"I'd really appreciate it if you did," she replied.

"Then I will," Malik said. "Being there will also help me get further along the investigation and you'll be one step closer to finding out if you have a sibling."

Even though the fact that the call had come from Ms. Bee's senior living home had caught Mya off guard, she smiled at being one step closer to finding out her past.

"Thanks for not keeping this information to yourself and waiting for us to have…" Her voice trailed off as she tried to get her words in order.

"You're welcome," he said as he gently touched her chin with his thumb. "I hope I didn't mess up your night." His eyes were filled with concern.

"Just the opposite," she said as she placed her wineglass on the table and leaned in closer to him. The moment their lips touched, she knew this was what she needed. There were plenty of unanswered questions still swarming around in her mind, but being with Malik, wrapped in his arms and kissing him slowly, just felt right.

Chapter 12

"You can do this," Mya said to herself as she walked into the senior living home with Malik right by her side. She shook out her hands as they made their way to the elevators. When they arrived at Ms. Bee's floor, Malik gently squeezed her shoulders.

"Are you okay?" he asked as they neared the room.

"I will be," she said giving him a slight smile. "I just hope I get some answers."

"You will," Malik replied. They knocked on the door.

"Mya, sweetie," Ms. Bee said as she opened the door, immediately pulling Mya in for a tight hug. She then glanced over at Malik.

"Who's this handsome fellow?" Ms. Bee asked as she winked at Mya.

"This is my friend Malik," she said as they walked into Ms. Bee's apartment. "He's working with me on the charity date auction."

"Ahhh," Ms. Bee said winging her finger in the air. "So you're the sexy cohost."

"Oh, really," Malik said, giving Mya a sly smile. "How sexy did she say I was?"

"Ms. Bee," Mya exclaimed as she took a seat on the sofa. "I never told you he was sexy."

"Oh yes, you did," Ms. Bee said taking a seat next to Mya on the couch. "After all these years I've learned to read between the lines with you. When you came in here wailing about how mad you were that you had to work with him, I could tell by your body language that you were attracted to him."

"And on that note," Mya said as she nodded for Malik to take a seat on the chair across from her and Ms. Bee. "I think I'll just get right down to business."

Ms. Bee jumped excitedly in her seat. "Oh my goodness," she said as her hands flew to her heart. "Are you two getting married? Will I finally get grandbabies? I'm getting too old and I want to play with my grandkids before I start losing my memory. And you aren't getting any younger," she said to Mya.

"Wait. What? Ms. Bee, that's not what I wanted to talk about," Mya said as her eyes grew big.

Ms. Bee looked from Malik to Mya. "So you aren't engaged?"

"No, not yet." She felt her entire face warm and could only hope that she wasn't blushing from embarrassment. "We're just friends, there are no plans to get engaged."

"Well which is it?" Ms. Bee asked in playful tone. "Either you plan on marrying the man or not."

Mya briefly wiped her hand over her forehead. She didn't even have to look at Malik to know he was enjoying her discomfort. His laugh told her as much. "Ms. Bee, this visit isn't about Malik and I."

"Then what did you want to talk about?"

Mya glanced over at Malik before she leaned closer to Ms. Bee and grabbed both her hands. "I have to ask you an important question."

"What is it?" Ms. Bee asked studying her face.

"Did you call—" she stumbled over her words and cleared her throat. She and Ms. Bee were extremely close and Mya knew that she would be able to take one look in the woman's eyes and know if she was telling her the truth or not. "Did you call me a few months ago to give me news about the possibility that I have a sibling?"

Ms. Bee didn't answer right away, but she didn't have to. Mya could read the truth in her eyes.

"Oh, Ms. Bee," Mya said as she let go of the woman's hands and ran her fingers down her face. "Why did you call me from a private number?"

Ms. Bee dropped her head and clutched her heart. "I didn't know how to tell you," she said as she lifted her head. "My friend's grandson knows how to do all that new-age technology stuff and he somehow blocked the call so that it couldn't be traced and had my friend call you and read from a script I wrote. I guess that didn't work."

"But why would you block the call?" Mya said, her voice rising slightly. "You could have just called me. How can you be so sure that I even have a sibling?"

Ms. Bee stood up and walked to her window, leaving Mya alone on the couch. When Ms. Bee's shoulders began moving up and down, she knew the older woman was crying. Mya shot Malik a concerned look before she walked over to Ms. Bee.

"Ms. Bee, what is it? What do you know about my past?"

Ms. Bee turned around and met Mya's curious stare. "Oh, sweetie," Ms. Bee said as she briefly touched Mya's cheek with the palm of her hand. "I would have called you myself, but I was too afraid to explain it to you after all these years, but I knew you needed to know. Meeting you at the women and children's shelter all those years ago wasn't an accident."

"What do you mean it wasn't an accident? We'd never met before that day."

"True, but I'd been sent to the shelter to find you," Ms. Bee said. "Although we'd never met, I knew your mother." Mya's eyes widened and her hands turned ice-cold.

"She was just a teenager when I met her and just like you, she grew up in the system. I'd met your mother at that same shelter more than twenty years before I found you there."

Mya opened her mouth to speak, but no words came out. *Ms. Bee knew my mother?* "How is it that you never told me this in all the years you've known me?" she asked finally finding her voice.

"Mya, I didn't tell you because I made your mom a promise that you would never find out about her."

"Is she still alive?" she asked, needing to know if her assumption was true.

"No, she isn't," Ms. Bee said as her eyes began filling with tears. "I received a call at the beginning of the year right before she passed. She knew her time was coming."

Mya closed her eyes tightly, refusing to cry over a woman she barely even knew. "She just passed away this year and you kept her secret all those years ago."

"I did, sweetie, but like I said, it was for your own good." Ms. Bee's voice cracked. "Your mother was one of the smartest people I knew so I wasn't surprised when she told me she'd landed her dream job and wouldn't be coming back to Chicago. She was always so focused on school that I barely saw her anyway. On one rainy day thirty years ago, I was headed for bed and got a knock on my door. I had just moved to a new neighborhood and didn't really know anyone. It was your mom and she was drenched, so of course I let her in. When I dried her off, she couldn't stop crying in my arms and I was so surprised because in all the years I'd known your mother, she never cried. When I asked her what was wrong, she told me that she couldn't talk about it, but that her career had forced her to give away her children."

"Are you sure she said children and not child?" Mya asked, the lids of her eyes filling with tears.

"Yes, dear, I'm positive. I hadn't seen your mother in years, so I hadn't even known she had kids. When I asked her what type of job would make a woman give up her children, she said that she couldn't tell me because it would put me in danger."

Ms. Bee scrunched her forehead. "That didn't sit well with me and before I convinced her to go to sleep, she finally told me that she worked for the government and in her line of work, people close to her would be in danger if she told them certain things. I didn't push any more that night and when I woke up in the morning, she was gone. Your mother always seemed so mysterious and although it hurt to only see her whenever she blew through the city, I had to accept it."

Mya began pacing back and forth, refusing to let the tears she was holding in slide down her face. "How did you find me?"

"Your mother actually found you," Ms. Bee said as she walked over to Mya. "Another time there was a knock on my door and it was your mother again. She gave me a quick hug, told me that she couldn't stay, but said that she had found her daughter and then she slipped a piece of paper in my pocket with the address to where I could find you. I immediately recognized the address as the same place I'd first found your mother when she was just a teenager. The odds that, years later, her daughter would end up in the same shelter, are uncanny. But I knew I had to follow your mother's wishes and see for myself if you were there."

Mya stopped pacing and stared at Ms. Bee. "She got a chance to see me?" Mya asked, her voice choking with emotion.

"She did, sweetie," Ms. Bee said as she wiped a few fallen tears. "She'd spent years trying to find you and when she did, she immediately came to me because she knew I would take care of you."

Ms. Bee placed her hand over Mya's and the warmth of her touch began immediately calming Mya's nerves. "When I met you at the shelter, I'd had a flashback of when I'd first met your mother. I could tell you'd had a hard life and it broke my heart to see the pain in your eyes."

"Meeting you was like a dream come true," Mya

said as she thought about the day she met Ms. Bee. "And now I know it wasn't an accident."

"It wasn't," Ms. Bee replied. "Your mother loved you very much. Although I would have loved you like my own grandchild despite who your mother was, there were a lot of gifts and other things that came from her that I had to pretend were from me. I also think it's important that you know that the anonymous scholarship that you received while you were in college was also from her."

Mya quickly swiped a tear as she thought about the scholarship she'd been informed that she received when she hadn't remembered applying for it.

"Mya," Ms. Bee continued. "I know you went through so much hurt growing up and trust me when I say that all I wanted to do for years was take that hurt away. But what you went through played a large part in molding the remarkable woman you are today. Although your mother couldn't raise you like she would have wanted to, when she found you, she did everything she could to make sure you felt loved the only way she knew how."

Mya glanced at Malik for the first time since Ms. Bee had began revealing the news. He gave her a supportive smile, his eyes promised not to leave her side unless she said so. "Thanks for telling me the story," Mya said to Ms. Bee. "Do you have a picture of her?"

Ms. Bee smiled and nodded her head. "Only one when she was about seventeen. I kept it hidden all these years, but now, I think it's time that I pass it on to you."

When Ms. Bee went in her bedroom to get the picture, Mya walked over to Malik, needing to feel his arms around her.

"I've never been the type of person that needed hugs," Mya said into Malik's chest as he stood and she soaked in his comforting warmth.

"Everyone needs a hug at some point," Malik said as he pulled her even closer. "Even a badass like yourself."

Mya gazed up at his face. "I'm pretty sure Princeton grads don't use naughty language like that."

Malik bent down to her ear. "If you thought that was naughty, you should hear how I chant the periodical table in the shower," he said with a grin.

Mya laughed aloud at his statement. "That was so lame."

"That may be, but it got you to smile."

"It did," she said as she continued to smile at him. "Thank you."

He placed a kiss on her forehead. "I'm proud of you." Mya sighed as she leaned back against his chest. She was sure they looked like a couple and she really didn't need to give Ms. Bee any ideas, but she couldn't help it. She was really beginning to rely on Malik in ways she'd never thought she would.

"Here is it," Ms. Bee said as she approached them. "It's a little old, but that was your mom."

Mya held the picture in her hand a little taken aback at the woman starring back at her. "We look so much alike," Mya said as her hands grazed over the picture. "I have her eyes."

"You sure do," Ms. Bee said with a smile. "You're the spitting image of her. A lot of the same personality traits too. Your mom was feisty and so sarcastic. People often tried to outwit her but failed every time."

"Sounds like someone else I know," Malik chimed in.

Mya looked at the back of the picture. *Kayla Anderson.* "Was that her name?" Mya asked as she pointed to the name scribbled on the back.

"Yes, it was," Ms. Bee said.

"Did she ever mention my father?"

"Not really," Ms. Bee replied. "On that same night she came to my house crying, I'd asked her if she was married or dating anyone. She'd told me that the father hadn't been in the picture and that it had been better for her children that way."

"What made you finally decide to call me that day?"

Ms. Bee gave Mya's hands a slight squeeze. "There was never really any way I could contact your mom and she barely called. When she did it was from an unknown number and I assume it was because she never wanted her calls traced. When she called me earlier this year, she sounded strange, so I knew something was wrong. She told me that she had beaten breast cancer twice, but that she wouldn't make it this time."

Malik handed Ms. Bee a tissue and she dabbed both eyes. "I hadn't even known she'd had breast cancer. But instead of sounding upset or defeated, she sounded liberated. Like she was glad she didn't have to live the life she had been living anymore. I could hear a nurse or doctor in the background saying that she had to hang up the phone, but she kept talking to me. She told me thanks for always being there for her and for taking care of you."

Mya swallowed hard when Ms. Bee didn't continue. "Is that all she said?" Mya asked, her voice barely above a whisper.

"No, that wasn't all." Ms. Bee took a deep breath. "The last thing she said before the line went dead was a little fuzzy because her voice was starting to slur, but from what I could make out, she said that her greatest achievement in life was getting a chance to see you grow into an adult and that she hoped one day you would be able to find your sister, Raina."

Sister... Mya looked from Ms. Bee to Malik. "So my mom had another daughter," she said more to herself than Malik. "After all these years, I have a sister."

Chapter 13

"Are you sure you need to get all this done tonight?" Malik asked Mya as they made their way to the largest conference room in the Ravinia Ranch Resort and Conference Center. The date auction was tomorrow and Malik and Mya had arrived early to make sure everything was in place.

Since they'd arrived, Mya had been working around the clock and Malik was worried that she was trying to keep busy as a distraction from what she'd found out two days prior.

"Stop worrying about me, Malik," Mya said as she continued to walk to the conference room. "I appreciate your concern, but it's not needed right now."

"Are you sure?" he asked. Mya stopped walking and turned to face him.

"Even though I've been on an emotional rollercoaster the last couple days, I learned that I had a mother who cared, a foster mother who proved she was always more than just a foster mother and somewhere out there in the world I actually have a sister."

She took a deep breath. "So to answer your question, no, I'm not 100 percent okay with suddenly finding out all this info, but the nervous energy that you are picking up on is not from what's going on with the case. It's the fact that this event is a do-or-die one for us. We have received a substantial amount of support for the after-school program, but I also hope we exceed above and beyond our goal today so that we can help out even more programs."

Malik studied her eyes and gently rubbed his thumb across her chin. "You are truly an amazing woman," he said speaking straight from the heart.

"I know," she said playfully. "That's what I've been trying to tell you."

"And there's the Mya I know," he said with a laugh.

"The Mya you know never left," she said as she started back walking. "I need this event to be perfect and I won't be able to sleep tonight if I don't make sure everything is flawless."

"Have you been having trouble sleeping?" Malik asked when they made it to the room.

"Yeah, I guess I have too much on my mind. That's why I'm making these last final touches in the room tonight, so that I won't have it on my mind when I go to sleep."

Malik watched Mya hop from random parts of the room checking on table setup and the stage, and then handling a variety of tasks in the corner of the room where items would be raffled off.

Watching her work was something he wasn't sure he'd ever get tired of seeing. He admired her work ethic and he was proud of the way she was handling everything since her talk with Ms. Bee. He'd expected her to shut down a little bit and possibly block him out, but she hadn't done that.

Time waits for no one. The conversation he'd had with Al Riviera echoed in his mind as he reflected on the excuse he'd given Al for not asking Mya out until after the event. They'd been spending a significant amount of time together, so in many ways he felt like they had already gone on several dates already.

Although he had no problem opening up to Mya about his past, there was a certain time in his life that he wasn't ready to talk about. A time in his life that often seeped into his dreams reminding him that no matter how much he tried to forget it, he couldn't. And he never would be able to.

A part of him felt like a hypocrite. He had allowed Mya to open up to him in a manner he doubted she ever had to anyone without being able to do the same to her. But somehow, he felt like saying the words out loud would push her away just as it had pushed away other women in his past.

"Okay, I think I'm done for the night," Mya said breaking his thoughts. He'd been so wrapped up in his own mind he hadn't even noticed her approaching him.

"Good thing. I thought we might be in here all night."

Mya lifted her eyebrows. "You didn't have to stay in here with me."

"If I didn't, we both know you would still be in here finding something that needs your attention."

Mya glanced around the conference room one final time. "You're probably right."

"I know I'm right," he said with a laugh. "So what are your plans for the rest of the night?"

"Let's see. I'll probably lay in bed, close my eyes, and pray I actually get some good sleep tonight."

As they stepped into the elevator, Malik pondered Mya's words. "Would you be up for a nightcap in my room?" he asked turning toward her. "I have a bottle of wine that I was saving for tomorrow night, but we could crack it open tonight."

She tilted her head to the side. "Sipping wine is supposed to be relaxing. You don't have something else you need to tell me tonight about the case, do you?"

He shook his head and laughed. "No, I don't. I figured since you've been having trouble sleeping anyway, and I don't plan on going to bed right away, we could spend that time together."

She turned one eyebrow in curiosity. "Doing what?"

Malik wondered if she could hear the rasping in her voice when she asked that. His eyes dropped to her lips.

"You'll find out when you get there," he said when the elevator arrived on the floor that his room was located. "But I promise, we won't do anything you don't want to do."

Malik was usually a very calculated thinker, but tonight, he wanted to lay all his cards on the table. He held his arm in the doorway to block the elevator from closing until he got an answer.

"I guess I'll come," she said when the door tried to shut for a second time. "I'll see you in ten minutes."

"See you then," Malik said as he finally let the door shut and proceeded to his room.

When they'd arrived at the resort and conference center, Malik had hoped they'd be on the same floor, or better yet, that they'd be stuck with connecting rooms again.

He wanted to give her a carefree night before the date auction. By the look on her face in the elevator, he was pretty sure she assumed that his solution to her lack of sleep would be something sexual. And she'd be right in assuming that. But Malik was a gentleman. Little did Mya know, he'd set up a late-night picnic in one of the gazebos on the resort ground that the owners had recommended.

He checked his watch and called the front desk.

"Hello. This is Malik Madden. I was told to call the front desk five minutes before I was ready to pick up the basket I had prepared."

"Thank you for notifying us," said the desk clerk. "We will have the basket waiting at the gazebo. Would that be all right?"

"Yes, that's perfect. Thanks."

After Malik hung up the phone, there was a knock on the door.

"You're a few minutes early," he said with a smile when he opened the door and then stood back to let her enter the room.

"I know," Mya replied. "Guess I didn't need the full ten minutes."

Malik noticed that she had reapplied some color

to her lips. She smelled good enough to eat and if he was lucky, he planned on doing just that.

Mya went over to the couch and took a seat.

"Actually," Malik said walking over to her. "Don't get too comfortable. We're about to head out."

She looked at him inquisitively. "Where are we going?"

"You'll see," he said with a sly smile.

"Um, did I forget to tell you I don't like surprises?" Mya said getting up from the sofa.

"Do you honestly think that will make me tell you where we are going?" Malik asked.

"I was hoping so."

"Not a chance. You'll just have to trust that it's a surprise you will like."

She shot him a doubtful look.

Her expression still remained when they passed the lobby and headed to the side doors that led outside.

"Uh, I don't follow people out into the dark without knowing where I'm going," she said as she stopped walking.

"This time you will," Malik said as he pushed her through the doors. "Now quit being so difficult and just follow me."

"What's the fun in being obedient?" she asked with a laugh.

"Didn't we just have this conversation not too long ago?" Malik asked rhetorically. "Sometimes, it's okay to be submissive."

"I remember our conversation," Mya said as they arrived at a dimly lit path that lead to the gazebo. Instead of a table and chairs, the staff had done a great job setting up a round wicker lounger with cream body cushions and large throw pillows. A standing wine chiller and two glasses were next to the lounger.

"Oh, wow," Mya said as they approached the gazebo. "This setup is gorgeous. Is this why you brought me out here?"

"Yes, it is," Malik said as he led her up the stairs to the lounger. "I figured you'd had such a long week and I wanted to do something special for you."

Mya began fiddling with her sundress as she looked around at the decor. *She's nervous*, Malik concluded.

"This is really beautiful," she said, looking anywhere but in his eyes.

"What's bothering you?" Malik asked.

"Nothing's bothering me," Mya said as she ran her fingers across the wine bottle. "I'm just surprised you did all this for me."

Malik walked over to her and caught her hand. "Don't be. You've been so stressed out lately and although the stress is warranted, you have to find time to take care of yourself and forget about everything else that's on your mind."

Malik lifted her chin so that she had no choice but to look into his eyes. "Tonight, it's all about you," Malik said as his lips got closer to hers. "You don't have to be strong and tough all the time, Mya. Let me take care of you for a change. Let me help ease your mind."

He watched the rim of her eyelids fill with unshed tears. He didn't want her to cry. The auction was tomorrow and Mya was the type of person who would be disappointed at herself if she let her emotions get the best of her before such an important day.

"You're fine," he said, hoping that she truly listened to his words. "Everything's fine." When she closed her eyes, he gently kissed both of her shut eyelids before lightly touching his lips to hers.

"Now," Malik said clasping his hands together. "I've been with you all night so I know you didn't eat dinner."

"Malik, I can't eat a full meal," she said placing her hand over her stomach as she sat on the wicker lounger. "My nerves are too bad and the last thing I need tomorrow is a stomachache."

"I knew you'd say that," Malik said as he went to the table in the back of the gazebo and grabbed the picnic basket the staff had placed there. "That's why instead of a full meal, we have a variety of cheeses, fruit and crackers for you to munch on. I figured it would be easier to convince you to eat this instead of dinner."

Mya glanced at the snacks and gave him a smile. "Is there anything you didn't think of?"

"Nope," he said with a confident grin as he opened the bottle of wine to pour them both a glass.

As they made their way back inside the resort, Mya couldn't believe how much better she felt. Everything that Malik had done was so sweet. She couldn't recall a man caring about her well-being the way he did.

She glanced at her phone and noticed it was 10:00 p.m. They had been talking under the gazebo for nearly two hours, although it hadn't even felt like that long. The responsible thing to do would be to return to her room and get some much-needed rest before the date auction. But she wasn't ready for the night to end and there was still no guarantee that she would go back to her room and actually be able to go to sleep. She looked up from her phone when she felt Malik's eyes on her.

"Tired of me already?" Malik asked, looking down at her phone.

"No, I'm not," she said as she tucked her phone away.

"That's good," he said studying her eyes. "I didn't want to have to finish the rest of this wine by myself."

She gave him a flirtatious smile as they stepped onto the elevator. "Why, Mr. Madden," she said, stepping closer to him when the doors had shut. "Are you inviting me back to your room for another nightcap?"

"That depends," he said as he ran his fingers up and down her arms. "Are you saying you want to come back to my room with me?"

She tilted her head to the side.

"I just want you to be sure that's what you want to do," he said as he continued to glide his fingers over her arms. "The decision is yours, but make no false pretenses, if you come to my room, the furthest thing on my mind would be talking."

Her skin felt hot enough to burn a hole through her clothes and she swore she saw steam coming from the sauna between her legs. When the elevator opened and Malik stepped out, he kept his eyes glued to hers, his thoughts visible and unyielding.

She tried to move her legs, but the predatory look in his gaze was holding her hostage in her spot. "You have to make a decision," he said stopping the elevator door again. "I'm afraid the next time it tries to close, it will signal a loud noise."

Malik was right and Mya didn't know what was wrong with her. She was always so witty and quick to come back with a statement. But she felt all those times she thought Malik was safe and boring were finally coming back to haunt her. The looks he shot her way were anything but friendly.

"Who said a nightcap had to involve talking?" she said, pushing him aside and exiting the elevator.

"Keep talking trash," he said with a smirk as he slipped his key card in the slot. "You'll need all that feistiness after I've had my way with you."

When Malik opened the door to his suite, she walked deeper into the room and shot him a seductive smile. "I'd like to see you try," she said as confidently as possible. "I may just have my way with you first."

She waited for him to say something back and when he didn't, she turned around to find his eyes locked to hers. *Oh man, why am I teasing him?* she thought as she tried to control her breathing. When he stepped to her, she stood her ground as realization hit that he would probably be the first man to ever make her so nervous that it rendered her speechless. And that thought scared her way more than she was willing to admit.

Chapter 14

"Sit down," Malik said firmly as he pointed to the sofa. She liked the more aggressive side of him and the daring side of her wanted to see what he would do next. Mya did as he asked right away and slid onto the sofa. She winced a little and tried to mask the pain she felt in her calves. Her muscles were extremely tight and for the umpteenth time today, she regretted her three-mile run yesterday evening.

"Are you okay?" Malik asked, not missing a beat. "I noticed that you've been occupied with your calves all day. Are they sore?"

When he came to sit on the couch next to her, she could've sworn her heart leaped to her throat. "I'm fine," she finally answered. "I went running yesterday and I'm not really a runner."

"Did you stretch before you ran?" he asked as he

ran his fingers down her legs to her feet before picking them up and placing them in his lap.

"Uh, no. I probably didn't stretch like I should have." She was trying to concentrate on answering his questions, but his hands on her legs were making it extremely difficult.

"Tsk, tsk," he said pointing a finger at her. "Running 101—always stretch out your legs and calves first." His finger outlined her left sandal before he slid the shoe off her foot.

"Did I ever tell you how much I like your toes?" he asked as he removed the other sandal.

"No, I can't say that you have," she said as she squirmed in her seat, anxious to have her foot back. When his fingers ran across the bottom of her feet she jumped and immediately began tugging her feet upward towards her chest.

"Nope, I told you what would happen if you came to my room," Malik said as he stretched her legs back over his lap. "You can't outrun me right now any more than you could outrun your thoughts yesterday."

Mya's head flew to his as she observed his steady gaze on hers. *Is there anything this man doesn't pick up on?* But he was right. Yesterday, she'd ran just for that reason. But all it had left her with were sore calves and an early appointment to her hairdresser's that morning to try and tame her unruly hair thanks to the Chicago rain that she'd also been caught in on her run back home.

"Do your calves and feet hurt?" Malik asked. She nodded, not trusting her voice to answer.

Slowly, he began kneading circles in her right foot, massaging out the cramps that had developed. His hands moved to her right calf, using the same technique he had used on her foot. Mya dropped her head back on the cushion and closed her eyes as she let herself enjoy the way his hands were making her feel.

"Does that feel good?" he asked as he moved to her left foot and calf.

"Amazing," she said, not daring to pretend that she wasn't enjoying every minute of it.

"Am I getting all the right spots?"

Oh man, was he! "Yes," she said as she held in a moan. "You're getting all the right spots."

"We'll see," he said before working both feet at the same time. Not only had Mya never received a foot massage before, but she also had never even let the woman who did her pedicures get this up close and personal with her feet. Malik knew how to work each and every muscle and before she knew it, she was in her own bubble of relaxing bliss. She was completely oblivious to how far up her dress had risen, nor did she realize that she was giving Malik his own personal peep show.

When she felt his slick tongue on her toe, she nearly jumped out of her skin. She lifted her head and opened her eyes to pull her toe away from his mouth, but she couldn't. It felt better than she was willing to admit.

"Malik," she said breathlessly as he worked her foot with his mouth and his hands.

"Hmm, you shouldn't have said my name like that."

She didn't have time to focus on what he was doing or even say anything in return. He had already left her feet and was traveling up her legs, settling on her calves. He twirled his tongue in circles on her thighs, continuing to massage her calves as he did so.

"Do you like how that feels?" he asked in between thigh kisses. She whimpered a sorry *yes*, unable to really formulate any coherent words. Her lack of speech seemed to prompt Malik to continue his plan to have his way with her body.

"Lift your legs for me, Mya," he said softly as he played with the edges of her lace panties.

She looked at her legs, one over his lap and the other spread across the top of the sofa, exposing all her goodies to the man stationed in between them. She dropped her head back to the sofa, and covered her face with her hands.

"Have you ever been this thoroughly satisfied?" The deepness of his voice made her toes curl. She felt her cheeks flush under the scrutiny of his gaze. "Now is not the time to get shy on me," Malik said as he began kissing her thighs again. "I've wanted to taste you since the first day I laid eyes on you and tonight, I plan to do just that. But if you want me to stop, now is the time to tell me."

Once again, Mya thought about how considerate Malik was about her feelings. Most men wouldn't even care at this point and would assume the next steps would be obvious. But not Malik. Not the man who had been surprising her since that night they met in his office and he handed her that contract that she'd wanted to burn the minute she saw it.

He was giving Mya a chance to back out. A chance to stop before they took it any further. *But why the heck would I say no to a man who looks like that?* Malik looked so sexy between her legs and she was way past the point of no return. She needed this release. She needed this release from him. And saying no was not an option. She slowly lifted her hips off the couch and sent up a silent thank-you to her hairdresser who had suggested she pamper herself. She'd just been able to squeeze in a bikini wax before she met Malik to head to the resort.

Malik gave her a sexy smirk before he began sliding her panties down her legs and tossing them to the side.

"Damn," he said aloud as he pushed her legs apart and gazed at her core as if it held all the answers to his problems. "You are one beautiful woman, Mya," he said as his lips traveled down her legs, up her thighs, and settled right where she wanted him to be.

He kissed her there softly at first, teasing her slowly before he dipped his tongue inside her in one quick swoop, catching her completely off guard.

Her hips bucked off the couch and not missing a beat, Malik caught her by the butt and pushed his tongue in even more. He took his time, dipping out of her center to suck on her clit, before returning to her center again. Mya couldn't hold back her moans anymore and soon she could hear her whimpers echoing off the walls.

When Malik briefly pulled away to adjust himself, Mya grabbed his head to keep him in place, riding his tongue in a way she'd never done before. Malik's hands were masterful. He worked his fingers in a way that made them dip in and out of her core at the same time his mouth continued to work her.

"Oh my goodness," she cried. "Malik. Malik. Malik." She was close to the edge of ecstasy and her first instinct was to scoot away from his tongue and fingers. But he must have known she was close too, because he held her in place.

As her heartbeat quickened and her muscles tensed with the pressure of a release soon to come, she had so many things she wished she had the guts to tell him. But she couldn't. She wouldn't. She was thirty years old and in her entire life, she'd never sexually had a real mind-blowing, leave-you-speechless kind of orgasm.

Giving a man the opportunity to perform any type of oral sex on her meant giving a man some of her control. Mya had spent a better part of her life deliberately refusing to give anyone any type of control over her and that included men in the bedroom. How could she tell Malik that although she'd had sex, she'd never allowed a man to make her this vulnerable? How could she tell him that she had never had a real orgasm?

Head back. Hair in disarray. Legs spread. She would have never predicted that she'd be in this predicament right now and all she could think about was how badly she didn't want it to end. Her stomach clenched and her legs locked. She knew it was coming and it was coming hard.

When she finally released her first real orgasm, Malik's mouth was still relentless against her core. Mya looked down at him between her legs as he lapped up her juices while massaging her thighs at the same time. When he lifted his head to hers, she didn't know what to say. Was she supposed to say thanks? Was she supposed to return the favor? She was sure there was some type of etiquette that she should be following, but she had no idea what that was.

"Can you stand up?" Malik asked.

"Um, I'm not sure," she said straightforwardly.

Malik stood up and before she knew what he was doing, he lifted her and placed her on the bed.

"What are you doing?" she asked as she watched his every movement. When he removed his shirt and revealed his amazing muscles and abs that she had dreamt about many nights, every rational thought she had was replaced by pure lust.

"I'm not done familiarizing myself with your taste yet," he said as he lifted her dress off and tossed it to the side with her panties.

Seriously? "I'm pretty sure you're familiar with my taste now."

He laughed as he dropped to his knees. "Not even close," he said as he slid her across the sheets until she collided with his face.

"Wrap your legs around my neck," he told her. "Unless you don't think I still need to familiarize myself with your taste."

It only took her a second to make up her mind. After what she'd just experienced on the couch, she wasn't sure if she would ever get tired of having Malik's tongue buried deep inside her.

"No," she answered as she wrapped her legs around his neck as he'd requested. "I think there's still more for you to taste."

As his tongue entered her again she ignored the little voice inside her head that told her that she could get used to coming home from work to a man like Malik everyday. He didn't even permanently live in Chicago so she knew it was a silly thought. But she feared she was already becoming addicted to him and she had no idea when it had happened.

"Obviously, I'm not doing enough to get you to stop thinking," Malik said in between licks. "Time to fix that. Hold on tight." She was just about to ask him why she needed to hold on when he lifted her off the bed and gripped her backside, her center still positioned right over his mouth.

"Oh crap," she moaned aloud as she sat on his shoulders so high up in the air she figured she could touch the ceiling if she wasn't too busy hanging on for dear life. He backed her up to the wall, but kept her positioned in the air as his tongue got to work.

The first orgasm had been amazing, but the spot his tongue was hitting right now was turning her into a ball of mush.

"What are you doing to me?" she breathed aloud before she could catch herself. He didn't answer with words, but he definitely answered with his tongue as he began lifting her up by her thighs just to bring her back down again.

Holy. Crap. She could no longer tell up from down, left from right. Front from back. She might as well just get a tattoo that said *Property of Malik Madden* with a downward facing arrow pointing to her vagina. There was no doubt in her mind that he owned it. Stamped it. Had engraved his initials in it with his tongue…literally and figuratively.

To have a mind-blowing orgasm on the couch was one thing. But to have one in midair with a man strong enough to lift you on his shoulders and keep you there while he tasted every bit of you was too much for any woman to handle. And she loved that the man performing such circus acts was Malik while she was the main attraction.

She finally realized that she could indeed touch the ceiling when an orgasm so strong hit her with brute force, causing her to try and hold on to something. Anything.

As one hand stayed on Malik's head and the other pushed to the ceiling, she shuddered the last of her release before collapsing on top of him. She only briefly recalled him catching her, placing her underneath the covers of the bed, and kissing her forehead. A kiss way too sweet for the erotic foreplay she'd just experienced.

Chapter 15

"Have you seen Mya?" Malik asked Micah when he caught him in the hallway.

"Yeah, I saw her earlier. Did you try giving her a call?"

"I tried, but she isn't answering." When Malik had woken up that morning, Mya wasn't in bed, so he knew she'd gone to her room. He'd gotten a message from her this morning saying that she couldn't make their breakfast meeting. All day, he'd been trying to corner her alone before the date auction. But he'd only gotten a chance to see her during the rehearsal with the candidates and the meeting they had with the volunteers and Elite Events staff who had all come out to support the event.

"I thought y'all were cool. Did something happen recently?" Micah asked.

Yeah, something happened. I gave her the best two orgasms she's ever had and now she isn't speaking to me. "Everything's fine," Malik said instead. "She's just being difficult."

"Well, I never thought I'd say this, bro," Micah said slapping him on the shoulder. "But if there is anyone who can get through to her it's you."

Malik laughed. "Thanks. I think."

"Yeah, it's a compliment," Micah said with a laugh. "I've never seen a man go toe-to-toe with Mya like you did at our house a couple weeks ago. But what I noticed the most was how into each other you both seemed to be. So whatever it is, I'm sure you can get through to her."

"I know," Malik replied. "I was just hoping we resolved this before the date auction."

"Try asking one of the ladies if they've seen her. Maybe Lex can help you corner her."

Just as Micah had suggested Malik go to Lex, he spotted her and Mya coming down the hallway. Malik nodded his head in their direction and Mya gave him a small wave before turning around and heading the other direction. Lex looked from Malik to Mya's retreating back before following after Mya.

"Hmm, on second thought," Micah said. "Maybe you should just wait until after the date auction. She's obviously avoiding you."

"We need to talk about this," Malik said with a frustrated breath. "I've spent too much time breaking down her walls for her to push me away now."

"Hold on," Micah said with concern. "This isn't about what I think it's about, is it?"

"Naw, man, I haven't even told her that yet," Malik said shaking his head.

"Why haven't you?"

"The timing hasn't been right. We've had a few serious conversations, but most of them have been about our childhoods."

"I get it," Micah said. "You've always been the type to help others and get them to open up about things. Though when it comes to things that hit you close to your heart, you avoid discussing it altogether."

Malik thought about what Micah had said. "Yeah well, past experiences with women taught me there's a time and a place for everything."

"True," Micah said nodding his head in agreement. "But Mya isn't those other women and the more involved you two become, the harder it will be for her to hear what you have to tell her. Being open and honest before things get too deep is the best way to handle this."

Malik saw something flicker in the corner of his eye and turned his head to find Al Riviera standing close by. Al lifted his cane and nodded his head in Malik's direction and on instinct, Malik nodded back before he remembered that Al couldn't see him.

"Oh man, I heard about him," Micah said as he followed Malik's gaze.

"Did I tell you that Mya and I had a conversation with him when we got stranded here?"

"Naw, you didn't. What did you talk about?"

Malik glanced over at Al who had diverted his attention to someone else. "We talked about a few things, but what stood out was the fact that he said he could tell I had a secret and that I needed to tell Mya."

Micah's head flew back to Malik. "He really said that?"

"Yeah," Malik said picking up on his brother's anxiousness. "Why?"

"Rumor has it, every now and then, he meets someone and he's able to feel their energy and hear their innermost thoughts and secrets."

"Get out of here," Malik said as he pushed Micah on the shoulder. "Like a psychic or something?"

"No, not a psychic. More like a telepathic, but it only works on certain people. He was in a terrible accident years ago. Although he survived, he became permanently blind and picked up a keen ability to read people's minds."

Malik glanced back at Al who was looking at him yet again. "Who told you this?" he asked Micah.

"One of the investors for M&M Security was telling Shawn and I about it in the office earlier this week when we mentioned the date auction. He was really convincing when he told his story."

"And you believe what he said?"

"I do," Micah said nodding his head. "Shawn did too. Our investor said he was at a conference here and he ran into Al at breakfast. Al sat and chatted with him and told him that he needed to make time for his wife and kids because they missed him. He thought Al was crazy of course, but after their conversation, he went home, told his wife and kids that he was taking them on a vacation that he had been meaning to take them on for years and that he was reducing his work hours to spend more time with them. On the vacation, his wife said she had planned to take the kids and stay with her parents after asking him for a divorce that very same day."

"But that could have just been a coincidence," Malik said.

"Could be," Micah replied. "But Al is blind, right?"

"Yeah, so?"

"Well look at him," Micah said pointing to where Al stood. "He's never met me and there are so many people standing around us, yet he's looking directly at you."

"He could be looking at anyone," Malik replied. As soon as the words left his mouth, Al walked over to them. "I was looking at you, Malik," Al said as he approached.

"Uh, I didn't. Um, what?" Malik's words stammered.

"I see you haven't taken my advice, but you need to soon. Time waits for no man and every woman deserves an honest man."

Malik looked from Micah to Al. "Did you hear our conversation from where you were standing."

"No, I didn't," Al said. "What I felt was in here," he said pointing at Malik's chest. "Listen to your brother. He knows what he's talking about," Al said, leaving a speechless Malik and Micah to watch his retreat.

"See, bro, I told you," Micah said as he clasped his hands together.

"I get it," Malik said. "I guess I better talk to Mya sooner rather than later."

"That's not what I'm talking about," Micah said as

he cuffed an arm over Malik's shoulder. "I'm talking about the fact that Al said you need to listen to me more. Being the older brother doesn't always mean you're right. If he can see it, I think you need to accept the fact that sometimes I'm smarter than you."

Malik looked at his brother and shook his head. "Out of everything Al told me, that's what you picked up on?"

"What?" Micah said as Malik began walking away. "Al recognizes greatness when he sees it," Micah yelled after him, but Malik was already halfway down the hallway determined to corner Mya.

Mya couldn't believe how many people were in attendance for the date auction. They had been hoping for five hundred attendees and had exceeded their goal by one hundred and fifty guests. They had even received late requests from a well-known journalist, a TV news anchor and a political activist who were each interested in being candidates in the date auction. Mya and her partners had decided to do three bonus mystery rounds to auction off the additional add-ons.

Between the donations, the money gained from the first twenty-five auctionees, and donations they'd received before the event, they had already raised well over $100,000, which was their original target goal.

Mya was also relieved that one of the biggest talk show hosts from Chicago was in town and offered to do some of the cohosting as long as he was able to get onstage with his childhood love who was also one of Chicago's other top radio hosts. It seemed that love was truly in the air, which begged Mya to ask herself the infamous question. Why in the world had she spent all day avoiding Malik?

"Are you finally ready to tell us why you keep avoiding Malik?"

Mya turned to find Imani, Cyd and Lex all standing on the side of the stage awaiting an answer.

"Guys, we still have ten more people to auction off plus the mystery candidates. Can't this conversation wait?"

"It could wait," Lex stated. "If we thought there was even a chance you'd have this discussion later."

"But now that you know we want to talk to you about Malik, we're pretty sure you'd avoid us after the auction just like you've done to him all day," Imani added.

"Besides," Cyd chimed in. "There are a lot of women here who have their eye on Malik so you may want to think twice about dodging him."

Mya turned back to the stage. "Malik is free to do whatever he wants with whomever he wants. If there's a woman here with her eye on him, great for her. Maybe we could auction him off too."

"You'd be pissed if that happened," Cyd said.

"No I wouldn't," Mya exclaimed. "If y'all are waiting for me to make some big declaration about how I feel about Malik, then it isn't going to happen. If a guy asks me out tonight I won't hesitate to say yes if he's attractive, so I don't expect Malik to feel any differently. We don't have any claims on one another."

Mya turned to gaze in her peripheral vision to find Malik standing with Daman, Shawn and Micah. He was watching her intently, listening to everything she was saying. *Just my luck...* It really didn't matter that he was there because she couldn't take back what she said.

When he approached them, the smirk he wore made her a little uneasy.

"So we don't have any claims on each other, huh?" Malik asked as he leaned his head closer to hers.

"That's what I said," Mya stated as she crossed her arms over her chest. "You're free to do whatever you please."

"Because we mean nothing to each other, right?" Malik said as he began walking around her slowly, purposefully.

"Exactly," Mya said not trusting herself to say more. "If circling me like a vulture is suppose to intimidate me, then you must have me confused with one of those weak-minded women you're used to dating."

Malik stopped walking and stood in front of her, his smirk still in place. Deep down, Mya didn't want to appear indifferent with him any more than she wanted him to appear unconcerned with her. But her feelings for him were moving at a much quicker pace than she was used to and she still hadn't took the time to fully comprehend what was going on between them.

Last night had not only been one of the best nights in her life, but she'd slept better than she had all year. The only person she had to thank for it was the man standing in front of her who she was purposely being rude to.

She hadn't meant for him to overhear what she had told her friends, but now that he had, she couldn't back down.

"This is a battle you stand to lose," Malik said as he crossed his arms over his chest as well. "Let's not pretend that this is about women in my past or men from yours. You're scared of this thing between us. And since you don't know how to handle it, you're lashing out and trying to push me away."

"Listen," Mya said stepping closer to him. "I'm not scared of anything."

"Oh yes, you are," he said with a laugh.

"No I'm not," she responded. "If you think after last night that somehow changes the way things are between us, then you're delusional." *Why in the world did I bring up last night?*

"Oh really," Malik said with a doubtful look. He leaned in even closer to her. "Last night I had you screaming my name in the sexiest voice I'd ever heard as you came harder than I bet you ever had before. And you haven't even begun to scratch the surface and see everything that I have to offer. When I woke up, you were gone and I know it's because the feelings you felt last night scared the crap out of you. But if you think for one minute that picking fights with me and pretending you don't care are enough to push me away, then you must have me confused with those pathetic men you're used to dating."

Hook. Line. Sinker. Malik walked away leaving her there to soak in his words and once again, Mya didn't have a comeback. Even worse, the entire charade had happened in front of her friends. At least the guys pretended not to hear the conversation. She couldn't say the same about her best friends.

"Well now," Imani said. "Is this the moment when

we pretend not to be curious about what happened last night? Or can we ask questions?"

"I'd hate to be you right now," Cyd said with a snarky smile. "You usually always have a witty response, but Malik just shut down all your defenses."

"Guess my soon-to-be brother-in-law isn't as boring and safe as you thought he was, huh?" Lex asked.

"Definitely not," she answered as she watched him waiting to go back onstage and announce the last date-auction candidates. When he turned around and caught her staring, he had the nerve to wink at her. He knew he'd won that argument and although she wanted to be disappointed that she'd lost the debate, she couldn't be. Standing there in his tailored suit, all she could think about was how amazing he would look if he weren't wearing anything at all. He looked sexy and confident. But even worse for her hormones, he looked all *strong male*.

Chapter 16

Malik made his way around the room, taking note of all the happy couples that were leaving the date auction. Whether they were winning bids for the auction, randomly matched singles paired together courtesy of Elite Events or people who'd made a connection for a lifetime or one night only, there was no doubt that the event had been a success.

The date auction had given awareness to individuals who may not have otherwise been concerned with the direction of the Chicago Public School after-school programs. But after tonight's event they were definitely aware of the struggles. The media exposure had shed some light on issues that Chicago educators and community leaders had been trying to reveal for years.

The night was finally coming to an end and Malik

was exhausted and per usual, he couldn't find Mya anywhere. He didn't want to retire to his room without talking to her first, but another quick scan of the room proved that she wasn't there.

As he made his way to his room, he couldn't help but reflect on the conversation they'd had earlier in front of their friends. Not only would Malik have rather discussed last night in private, but he also didn't want to call her out in front of everyone. But he was learning that when it came to Mya, the only way to get her to see reason sometimes was to have a discussion publically. Cornering her privately when she didn't want to be found was way more difficult than he'd ever imagined and he'd made a living on finding out details and people who didn't want to be found.

His mind drifted to the investigation as he thought about his recent findings. He didn't want to talk to Mya about anything until he was sure, but he believed he had a lead as to where her sister was located. But he'd have to do some more digging before he brought that to her.

When he stepped off the elevator and walked into his room, he immediately stopped in his tracks. *Someone else is in here.* His senses never failed him. In his line of work, he always had to be careful and although he chose his clients carefully, the people he had to track down were sometimes involved in some shady business. He quickly sent a vague text to Shawn and Micah that he knew they would understand.

The safe was located in the front closet door, but he wasn't sure where the person was in his room. He decided to pretend to be talking to someone in the hallway to mask the sound of the safe opening. When it did, he pulled out his pistol and continued to talk as he clicked off the safety. When he'd checked in, he was glad to get a suite and had appreciated Al and his son Vero giving him and Mya two of the best suites in the resort. Now, the extra rooms just added extra space he needed to check for the intruder. After he cleared the living room and kitchenette, he knew the person was in the bedroom or bathroom.

Rounding the corner, he peeped through the crack of the bedroom door and saw a shadow standing by the room.

"Turn around slowly," he said, his breath catching in his throat as the intruder did.

"Um, do you always greet a half-naked woman with a gun?" Mya said as she put her hands in front of her face. Malik barely had time to register what she had said because he was too caught off guard by the light yellow lace bra and panty set with sexy silver stilettos she wore to even realize that he still had his gun pointed at her.

"Malik," she said with her hands still up. "Do you think that maybe you could admire my lingerie without the pistol?"

"I'm so sorry," Malik said putting the safety back on and sticking it in the back of his pants. "I thought you were someone else?"

"Let me guess," Mya said as she cracked her neck. "Flashbacks of your FBI days? You know, if Cyd and Lex hadn't told me about similar circumstances with Shawn and Micah, I'd really be freaked out right now."

Shawn and Micah. "Don't you move," Malik said as he held out his hands to Mya. "I'll be right back."

He rushed out the door and found Shawn and Micah in the hallway. "False alarm, guys."

"Yeah, we know," Shawn said. "We'd gotten to the living room when we recognized Mya's voice. We just wanted to tell you we were headed back to our rooms."

"I think you can handle Mya without us, bro," Micah said with a laugh. After they left and Malik placed the pistol back in the safe, he was glad to find Mya hadn't moved. But he did notice her phone and Bluetooth speaker on the nightstand playing seductive R&B music.

"Have you secured the premises, Agent Madden?" Mya said with a flirtatious smile.

He walked over to her and touched the bottom of her chin. "I'm sorry I pointed my pistol at you. Are you sure you're okay?"

"I'm fine," she said as she wrapped her arms around his waist. "Seeing you look all FBI-like was kinda sexy."

He let his eyes travel the length of her. "I think you're pretty sexy."

"And you have on way too many clothes," she said as she began taking off pieces of his suit while he kicked off his shoes. "I've been waiting to take you out of this thing all day." She placed soft kisses along his bare chest before gliding down his body to unbuckle his pants. Malik watched her squat in front of him thinking he'd never seen anything so sexy in his entire life.

She slowly dragged his pants down his legs, followed by his underwear. He watched her eyes grow big as she took in the length of him, which was standing to attention. She gazed at him and sashayed back up to the beat of the music, the fire in her eyes even more prominent than before.

"Lie on the bed," she requested just as firmly as he'd requested things from her the night before. He obeyed her request and lay in the middle of the bed.

Mya sleeked up his body with the finesse of a jaguar that'd just landed eyes on its target. He didn't know what part of her body to focus on. The seductive curve of her back. The roundness of her butt. The way her wavy hair all flowed to one side of her face. The way her calves looked crossed over one another accentuated by the heels that he'd already decided he wanted her to keep on.

For a man who prided himself on his patience, Malik was feeling anything but patient at the moment. The need for him to be inside her was reaching an all-time high the more she rolled her body over his. When her hands wrapped around his shaft, it took all his focus to remember that he wanted the first time he came to be buried deep inside her, not her hands.

"I've never tasted one before," she said softly.

"You don't have to do anything you don't want to do," Malik said as he watched her observe him.

"That's not it," she said as she began rubbing him up and down. "I want to, I just want you to know that I've never done it in case I'm not the best."

"That's not possible," he said looking down at her. For a woman as bold and feisty as Mya, she was having a shy moment. He knew it was hard for her to tell him that she'd never tasted a man before, so he knew he had to ease the situation for her.

"Mya, we have plenty of time for you to work up

to that if you choose so in the future. What you're doing with your hands is already about to bring me to the brink."

She looked at him, then she looked at the tip and lightly swirled her tongue around it. When she received a response from him, she sucked him into her mouth even more and alternated from fondling him and rubbing his shaft. The combination caused him to groan aloud. The noise caused her to look up at his face, but she didn't remove him from her mouth right away and when she did release him, she bit her bottom lip before dipping back down. *Sexiest. Look. Ever.* If Malik could take that look and bottle it to look at it whenever he pleased, he would do just that.

Once she sucked him whole in her mouth, he almost lost all ability to think. Wisps of her hair traveled over his midsection as her mouth moved up and down. Quicker. Faster.

"Mya," Malik called in between groans. "Mya," he called again when she didn't let up. When she only quickened her movements more, he realized that she wasn't going to show him any mercy, so if he wanted to come inside her for the first time, he had to take control of the situation.

Malik sat up in the bed, grabbed Mya by the arms, and slid her up his body. With every wicked squirm of her hips, he cursed at his body for not understanding why he'd stopped her.

"I was just having fun," she said with a naughty smile.

"I know you were," Malik said as he flipped her on her back. "If I'd let you have any more fun, this night would end entirely too early."

He kissed her neck before trailing kisses down her body, stopping along the way to remove her bra and panties. When he had her completely naked, spread out across the bed, he admired every crease and crevice of her body, taking a mental image of a woman he was confident would be completely and utterly his one day.

He wasn't sure why he'd always known that Mya would be his, but he had. And ever since the first day he met her, he knew he had to treat her differently than he had other women. Malik had never been the type to date multiple women at once or anything like that, but he also hadn't always put as much effort forth as he should have. In his past relationships, he'd always felt like something was missing. The women he had dated were either extremely smart and willing to mold themselves into the type of woman they thought he had wanted. Or they were all beauty, little brains. And then there were the women who had already began planning their wedding after one date. Or the women who never seemed to show any other type of emotion except for a positive, upbeat personality all the time.

Nothing was wrong with those women, but they weren't for him. They weren't the type of woman he wanted to build a life or foundation with. In all circumstances, his exes lacked depth and complexity. And although people met him and assumed that his careful and cautious approach meant he wanted a mild-tempered type of woman, they were sadly mistaken.

There had been a couple women who he had thought might be the one he was meant to be with, but any woman who couldn't accept all of him, flaws and all, wasn't the type of woman for him.

Mya was perfect for him and even though she hadn't realized it yet, he felt like she had been carved out just for him. He bent down and kissed her with all the emotions he felt but couldn't yet share. She kissed him back just as passionately, her moans driving him to grab a condom from the nightstand, happy he'd had the foresight to bring protection just in case.

His fingers slinked past her folds as he checked to see if she was wet enough for him. The act quickly turned into more when she responded to his two fingers by tightly clenching her muscles. He moved his fingers in an upward rotation, rewarded by her pumping her body to meet him thrust for thrust. Once he had her on the edge, he removed his fingers and slowly slid inside her wet center, allowing her to get comfortable with his length.

She moaned into his ears the moment he filled her completely.

"Is that okay?" he asked, knowing it was a lot to get used to the first time.

She looked at him through glazed over eyes. "It's perfect," she said as she began rotating her hips the same way she had on his hands. "How does it feel to you?" she asked.

"Amazing," he said in between thrusts.

He looked down at her and noticed a sneaky look on her face. "What are you up to?" he asked as he looked at the ceiling and tried to maintain control.

"Nothing," she said with a moan. "I was just thinking that you seem to be perfectly made to fit inside me." His eyes flew to hers.

"Don't you think so?" she said breathlessly. "The way my juices flow down your shaft as my vaginal muscles clench with every motion you make."

"Oh damn," he groaned. He knew what she was doing. She was taking back control of the situation by talking dirty to him…and she was winning.

"I bet it felt good to have my tongue wrapped around your tip," she said as she met his thrusts even harder.

He lifted her right leg and threw it over his shoulder as he slid her left leg between his so that she was facing sideways. If she was going to talk him over the edge, there was no doubt in his mind that he was bringing her along for the fall.

Within seconds, no more words were spoken and the only sounds in the room were their moans and groans mingling with the slight creak of the bed. Malik was close and luckily, he felt that Mya was close too.

He turned her leg slightly more to the ceiling and knew the exact moment he had locked and loaded. After three more thrusts, she released an orgasm so hard that his immediately followed, causing them to connect in an unworldly wave of pure ecstasy.

"Wow," Mya said after Malik had collapsed on the side of her.

"Wow works for me," Malik said as he turned to his side to view her. He propped his head on his elbow and sucked her nipple into his mouth.

"You can't seriously be ready to go again," she said with a laugh.

"Wrong," he said mischievously.

"Why are you always saying I'm wrong?"

"Why do you always think you're right?"

"Because I am," she said with a slight shrug.

"Wrong again. I'm ready to go again," he said bringing his lips to her breasts. "And you have no idea what you're in for." He sucked her other nipple in his mouth. Minutes later, all laughter ceased as Malik showed her what it felt like to be with a sexually insatiable man.

Chapter 17

Mya stepped out of the car and admired the cozy lake house nestled in between a group of trees that offered a bit of privacy from the neighbors.

"Um, exactly how many places do you live? You've already shown me two properties other than this one."

Mya walked over to Malik who was getting their bags out of the trunk. It had been two weeks since the date auction and after that night they'd spent together in the resort, they'd been together almost every night since. His condo in Hyde Park, not far from downtown Chicago, was really nice and equipped with a pool and fitness center. Mya had spent a couple nights there, taking advantage of the amenities.

When he'd asked her to go with him to Detroit for the weekend, it hadn't taken long for her to say yes. But he had failed to mention that they would only briefly be stopping at his condo in Detroit. Instead, they'd driven about an hour and a half out of Detroit to a small lake town.

"The only other properties that I have that you haven't seen are in Arkansas."

Mya raised an eyebrow at him. "Properties as in more than one."

"Yes," he said with a laugh as he they made their way up the stairs of the lake house. "My brothers and I invested in a building in Little Rock and I also invested in a home in Cranberry Heights. I usually rent out all my properties except the penthouse of my building in Chicago and my condo in Detroit."

"So this location is not usually vacant?" she asked as he opened the door.

"No it's not, but I don't have anyone staying here for another few weeks, so I figured it would be a perfect minivacation."

He opened the door and gestured for Mya to step in. The first thing she noticed when she walked through the door was the modern wooden furniture and massive fireplace. She took a deep breath as she moved into the living room. "I love that smell," she said as she followed the scent to see where it was coming from.

"It's clove and cinnamon with a hint of ginger," Malik stated as he placed their bags down. "When I was initially looking to purchase a lake house, I couldn't believe how many places the Realtor showed me that were stuffy or musky. My mom is constantly making oils and fragrances for the home, so I had her create a scent for the lake house. Even though it's time for me to swipe out the old oil, you can tell how long the smell lasts."

Malik showed Mya the rest of the lake house, including the large oversized wooden deck in the backyard, and the customized wooden balcony on the second floor that overlooked the lake.

"It feels like no one can see us when we're up here," Mya said as she walked to the railing.

"That's because they can't," Malik said as he walked over to join her. "Check this out," he said as he grabbed her hand and walked to the side of the balcony to a set of stairs.

"Where do these stairs lead to?" she asked as she followed him. Large trees sat on either side of the balcony. Mya was in such awe of the fact that they were walking up wooden stairs through a set of trees, that she almost missed the perfect sight that came into view when they reached the top of the trees.

"Oh my goodness," she said as she looked into the sky and twirled around in a circle. The sun was beginning to set and colored the sky in an array of warm orange, red and yellow colors. The top of the large trees cascaded over the top layer of the balcony and offered a secret view to the lake.

"We can see other houses," Malik said coming to stand near her. "But the neighbors can't see us because we're nestled in the trees."

"How in the world did you come up with this idea?"

"I didn't actually," Malik said. "A friend of mine works for this company that specializes in building tree houses. They also have a show on television."

"Oh man, I think I've seen that show," Mya exclaimed.

"You probably have. It's on the home network

channel. They were in Michigan building tree houses for two families and I asked him to shoot on over and take a look at these trees and tell me if there was anything I could do. The trees were really the main reason I settled on this house. I knew it would be perfect for a balcony and large deck, but I never imagined having this add-on. The only thing I have to battle up here are the birds and squirrels who like to drop by from time to time."

Mya laughed at his comment as she walked over to the edge of the railing. "This is so peaceful," she said as the wind caught in her hair and whipped in the wind.

"I'm glad you like it," Malik said. "I was really hoping you liked it."

"What's not to like?" she said as she pulled her hair to one side. "It's beautiful. Have you ever brought another woman up here that didn't like it?" she asked. He glanced at her before leaning over the railing.

"No," he said looking back at her. "I had every intention on bringing my last girlfriend up here. But she never made it past the front door."

"Why is that?" Mya asked. "She didn't want to spend time here?"

"It wasn't the lake house," he said as he gazed back out into the water. "We had an argument right before we arrived and when we got here, she asked me if I could bring her back home. We broke up soon after."

Mya leaned down so that she was aligned to Malik on the railing. "Is this the same woman you brought to Imani and Daman's wedding years ago?"

Malik gave her a side smirk. "One and the same."

She watched the range of emotions cross his face

and something about his look was a little unsettling. *Does he still love her?* She'd heard they'd been together for a while and although she'd never given her heart to someone, the tone in Malik's voice proved to her that he had.

"I don't still love her if that's what you're thinking," Malik said, interrupting her thoughts.

"Why did you two break up?" Mya asked.

Malik looked from her to the lake again. After a few minutes of silence, Mya figured he didn't want to talk about it.

"I remember my first day in seventh grade, I had no idea that my teacher's introduction would have stayed with me all these years. This teacher probably impacted me the most."

His voice trailed off and Mya tried to piece together what his schooling had to do with his previous relationship.

"My school in Little Rock didn't have the best academic record at the time and my teacher was trying to get the class to understand the importance of education," he continued. "He divided us into four groups and then told us that out of the four groups, one group wouldn't graduate eighth grade next year."

"That's intense for a group of seventh graders to hear," Mya replied.

"It was," he said nodding his head. "But he needed to be frank in order to reach at least one student in that class. When he took a good look at the three remaining groups, he said only one group would graduate high school. Then out of that last group, he pulled two students aside and said only two students would actually make it to college and neither would attend graduate school."

"Sounds like a good scare tactic," Mya said as she turned to face him.

"It definitely worked on me," Malik continued. "The last thing he asked us to do was look around the room at our classmates. Some students just laughed it off, some seemed indifferent to the exercise and a few students, like me, actually took a good look around the room at every student. He said at least five students would be killed before their sixteenth birthday."

"He liked to make an impact," Mya stated.

"He was a realist," Malik added. "His point was to say that those were the statistics based off of previous students, but that it was up to us to beat the odds. Society wanted us to fail and even with the cards stacked against us, it was in our power to succeed if given the right tools and that's what he wanted to do."

"What group did he place you in?" Mya asked.

"Everyone in the class knew I had the best grades, but he'd divided us randomly, so it wasn't based off your rank in school." Malik glanced over at her before continuing. "I was in the group that got eliminated first. That was the day I decided that no one would ever be able to pick me from a crowd and choose my destiny."

Malik glanced up at the sky before asking her if she wanted to sit by the lake before the sun went completely down. As she observed his behavior, she wondered what else was on his mind since he seemed to be deep in thought.

"That was a really enlightening story," Mya said as they took a seat side by side on the edge of the wooden dock leading to the lake. "I imagine it somehow ties into your relationship with your ex."

"It does," Malik said as he leaned back on the palms of his hands. "That was also the same year my dad managed to get me my first bike. I drove that bike everywhere and it offered me my own escape of reality. A way of leaving my world and experience other neighborhoods and different cultures. I refused to be another statistic and I didn't care that my feet barely touched the petals because I knew I'd grow into it one day. I fell in love with cycling so when I got to college, I decided to enter my first bike marathon."

"That seems exciting," Mya stated as she curled one leg under the other and turned to face him instead of the water.

"The thrill I got was amazing and when I cycled, everything and everyone disappeared. It was me and my own world that I'd created."

"Do you still compete in marathons?" Mya asked. She watched the lit expression he wore on his face dim the minute she asked the question.

"Not anymore," he replied. "After my first marathon, I was able to compete in two more before I was in a biking accident during my fourth marathon."

"Oh no," Mya said as her hand flew to her chest. "How did that happen?"

"Some idiot didn't pay attention to the road block. He'd also been drinking in the middle of the day. Turns out, he'd just lost his job and his wife on the same day."

"Were you okay?" Mya asked as she lightly placed her hand over his.

"Two broken ribs, a sprained arm, a broken leg and bruises all along my body."

"That's terrible," Mya said as she scooted closer to him. "But it could have been much worse."

"It did get much worse," he said as he leaned up and faced her. She studied his eyes as she waited for him to continue. When he dropped his head and lifted it back to hers, she could see the emotion in his eyes.

"At the time, as I began to heal, I thought I was fine. My ribs began to heal, the bruises started fading and my leg was beginning to feel better despite what had happened. It wasn't until seven years later, that my girlfriend at the time, who I'd planned on proposing to suggested we get checked out."

Mya's heartbeat quickened at a rapid pace, as she waited for him to continue. It was hard not to react to Malik's nervous energy, which caused her anxiousness to increase.

"She knew I was close to proposing as well and she wanted us to be aware of what lied ahead. She was always prepared like that so we went to a fertility clinic together and that's when I learned that the chance of me having children of my own was extremely slim."

Mya's hand clenched at her side at the look of distress on his face.

"I'd experienced some testicular damage during my biking accident resulting in poor sperm motility. So basically, my sperm is sluggish which makes it harder for me to fertilize an egg."

Reacting on instinct, Mya got on her knees and lifted herself on top of Malik and encased him in her arms. "And your ex left you because of that."

"Yes," he said with a sigh. "Both my exes did. Each

woman wanted a guarantee that they would bear children and neither was willing to look into opportunities beyond the old-fashioned way."

He finally wrapped his arms around her and returned her hug. "Can you believe it?" he said with a slight chuckle. "The one activity that helped me escape from the hardship of my neighborhood was the exact same thing that caused my inability to fertilize a child."

"God has plans for each of us," Mya said as she gently cupped his face with both hands. "You can't look at this like a burden, but instead, an opportunity to possibly make the life better for a child who would benefit from having you as a parent. Take it from someone who used to pray she got adopted. There is plenty of love you can give a child without a home and those women who left you didn't see what I see…a man willing to do anything for a family of his own."

Her eyes watered when she saw the relief in his gaze and she returned to hugging him as he rested his head on her chest. In that moment, she knew in the pit of her stomach that she was falling hard for Malik Madden.

"Is that something you could handle? Not bearing your own children?"

She squeezed him even tighter. "I knew a long time ago that even if I bore children of my own, I also wanted to adopt. I'm okay if adoption is the only option."

Mya knew that her statement was the most she'd insinuated to a future with him since they'd begun spending time together. She'd spent this entire time appreciating his support, but believing that he didn't really understand how it felt to not feel wanted when it turned out he'd been rejected twice for something that was completely out of his control.

As they sat on the dock, the bright moon rising to replace the fallen sun, she thought about how her life would be if she were to marry Malik. They hadn't expressed their feelings for one another, but if they were meant to be together in the future, she knew for a fact that walking away from Malik was not an option.

Chapter 18

Malik patiently watched Mya take a bite of her chicken before picking up her glass to get a sip of water.

"Are you going to keep staring at me all night?" she asked.

"Probably," he said with a smirk as she resumed eating. He had been stealing glances at her for the past thirty minutes as he waited for her to finish her meal. He'd taken her to his lake house with the intention of telling her the secret he'd been harboring, but he hadn't known the right time to do so.

When they'd started talking outside upon arriving at the lake house, the window of opportunity presented itself and he took a chance and opened up to her. The response he'd received had touched him more than Mya probably realized and had been just what he needed to solidify his feelings. There was no more denying it. He'd fallen in love with Mya, and his feelings felt so strong that he questioned his prior serious relationships, no longer confident that what he'd felt for them was that deep hit-you-in-the-middle-of-your-gut type of love.

Mya was the real deal. The type of woman a man rarely found and he was confident that she felt the same way although they hadn't shared their feelings with each other yet.

"I'm finished," she said as she wiped her hands on her napkin and lifted her plate from the table. When she made it to his side of the table, she reached down to pick up his plate, when he lightly gripped her wrist.

"Leave it," he said as he took her plate out of her hands and placed it on top of his.

"I thought we were going to watch a movie," she said looking down at him. He released her wrist and stood up in front of her.

"The last thing on my mind is a movie," he said looking her up and down.

Her eyes trailed over his body and stopped right at his midsection. "I guess you're right," she said, gently cupping him through the fabric of his pants. "A movie is the last thing on your mind."

"Glad we're on the same page," he said before he scooped her over his shoulder and began walking up the stairs.

"Is there a reason why you always lift me in the air?" Mya asked with a laugh.

"Maybe if you didn't make things so difficult, I wouldn't have to lift you in the air."

Even upside down, he felt her brain processing his

words. "Oh," she said. "Well in that case, I guess I better not make things too easy for you."

"Somehow I doubted you would," he said with a laugh. When they arrived at the second floor, he opened the screen door to the balcony and placed her on her feet.

"Come on," he said as he led her up the stairs to the second balcony level in between the trees.

"It's a little chilly out here," she said with a shiver as she observed the large gray clouds above them. "And it looks like it's about to rain."

"Then we'll just have to create our own heat." Malik took off his shirt and threw it on the corner of the balcony. His pants quickly followed. "Your turn," he told her as he took a seat on the lounge chair he'd brought up while she had showered earlier.

"Evidently, you had all this planned out, huh?" she asked when she noticed he was wearing protection. She began giving him a mini striptease as she removed her clothing, purposefully moving very slowly.

"I'm done waiting," he said pulling her closer to him and kissing her fiercely. He turned her around so that her back was to his chest and lifted her up, gently gliding her down onto his cock. When he was completely inside her, he groaned in satisfaction.

Mya wasted no time moving up and down his length, gripping his legs tightly as she slipped him in and out of her wet center. He kneaded the bead of her clit with his thumb, taking advantage of the backwards angle Mya was positioned in.

As their moans increased, so did their pace. "I've dreamed about making love to you on this balcony for weeks," Malik said in between thrusts.

Mya didn't respond, but instead, she rotated her hips in a way he'd grown to love over the past couple weeks, pushing him closer to his breaking point. When she bent over, giving him an unrestricted view of her butt as she continued to gyrate on top of him, Malik almost lost it right there as the seductive image glared back at him. He didn't want to do something reckless like express his love to her in the middle of sex, but the way she was moving her body made him want to spit out all types of sentimental words of adoration.

When she sputtered a high-pitched moan, he knew she was close, so he stood up and grabbed her by the waist as she locked her legs around him backwards. Malik never rehearsed the moves in his mind of what he would do to Mya, but he appreciated the fact that she always caught on quickly no matter how insane the sex position was.

"If you drop me, I'm going to hurt you," she said in between thrusts. She really had nothing to brace herself on but his forearms, so he swung around to the railing to offer her a better grip. When he did, it brought him even deeper inside.

"Mya," he said in one breath hoping she picked up on the strain in his voice. When she rotated her hips again, he knew she had and within moments they both succumbed to a passionate orgasm.

As Mya regained focus and her orgasm subsided, she allowed Micah to lower her back onto the wooden floor. She turned around to face him, noticing that he was still coming down from his high as well.

He pulled her into his arms and held her close.

Mya buried her head in his chest, as they stood there, naked and satiated, just enjoying the feel of being in each other's arms. It wasn't just a simple hug between lovers. What she felt in his embrace was so much more.

Mya lifted her head when she felt beads of water slide down her exposed back.

"Do you want to go back inside before it starts pouring?" Malik asked.

She glanced at the chair before glancing back at him. "Not really," she said bringing him back over to the chair. "Take a seat." He looked at her inquisitively before taking a seat in the lounger.

She purposely backed away from him to take in her fill of his sexy body draped across the chair. "I've always wanted to do this." Gradually, she made her way to him and eased on top of him so that she was sitting on his lap seated face-to-face and chest-to-breasts.

As the rain began to fall, she moved her hips to the sound of the raindrops hitting the wooden balcony. Mya had never been much for looking into a man's eyes when they had sex. But with Malik, she felt inclined to hold his gaze as she moved on his shaft, clenching her vaginal muscles with every in and out movement.

Malik gripped her butt and moved his hips to meet her movement. Before, they'd been so hungry for each other the sex had been raw. Passionate. *Obsessive.* Now, she wanted to savor the moment and show her appreciation for having him in her life without necessarily voicing those words.

She hated to sound cliché, but making love to him

made her feel alive. When they connected in the most intimate way possible, she felt more united with him than anyone from her past or present. Malik knew her. The real her. And although the idea of giving her heart to him scared her like crazy, the truth was that he already had her heart in the palm of his hand. And instead of turning his back on her or expecting her to fit in this perfect box of society's definition of the ideal woman, he allowed her to be herself.

For her entire life, Mya had avoided any topics that made her emotional for fear that once the tears started flowing, she wouldn't get them to stop. But Malik had forced her to come face to face with her biggest fears, and even though she didn't know if her investigation would have a happy ending, she wouldn't regret going to Malik for his expertise. In doing so, she'd not only learned a lot about her past, but she'd also opened up to an amazing man who she may not have ever opened up to if the circumstances had been different.

Overcome with emotion and no longer wanting to hold it in, she dropped her head back and allowed the water hit her face and flow down her body. The refreshing rain shower mingled with the salty tears that cascaded down her face. Malik must have sensed her nearing an orgasm, because he rolled his hips forward, hitting her sweet spot.

She brought her forehead to his as all thoughts ceased to exist the moment they let their release flow from their bodies, resulting in the sweetest moment Mya had ever experienced in her entire life.

When she lifted her head to meet his eyes, it seemed that neither cared that the speed of the rain had increased. Malik touched the tip of her chin and pulled her lips down to his in a tender kiss.

"I love you," Malik said, his hand still on her chin. "In my mind, I always pictured I'd first say those words to you at a candlelit dinner or something romantic like that."

Mya leaned closer to Malik. "You know what," she said, touching her forehead to his. "I think saying those words in the middle of an unpredictable rainstorm is pretty fitting of our relationship so far."

She gave him a soft smile. "I love you too," she continued as she slipped her tongue between his lips in a loving kiss filled with promises and unpredictability.

Malik glanced over at Mya who was sleeping soundly in the bed, one leg entangled in the sheets and the other uncovered for his viewing pleasure. Yesterday had been amazing and after making love all night, all he wanted to do was lie next to her in bed all day and do it all over again.

He looked back at his laptop on his desk as he analyzed the information he'd finally pieced together. After finally expressing their feelings for one another, the last thing he would have expected to have to do today was talk to Mya about the investigation. When he opened the last file he'd uncovered, his breath caught in his throat. *What the hell?* He had to be reading it incorrectly.

He clicked on a few more files, each resulting in the same conclusion.

"What are you doing up?" Mya asked.

Malik turned to her quicker than he'd originally

planned. *There is nothing sexier than a naked woman wrapped in a snow-white sheet*, he thought with a satisfied smile on his face. *Now is not the time for that*, he warned himself.

"I had to check something out," he stated. She squinted her eyes and turned her lips to one side.

"Does this have something to do with my investigation?" she asked. He didn't answer right away.

"Judging by that look on your face, I assume I'm right."

"You are," Malik said as he exited out of a few screens and shut his laptop. "But we can talk about that after you take a shower."

"I'd rather talk about it now," she said getting off the bed and wrapping her body in the sheet. "What did you find out? Did you find my sister?"

Malik scratched the back of his head still unsure if now was the time for this conversation.

"Malik," she said walking to him and sitting on the edge of the bed. "What is it?"

He let out a deep breath, knowing that she wasn't going to let him prolong this conversation. "Yes," he stated. "I found your sister."

"You did," Mya said nervously. "What did you find out?"

"For starters," he said, raising the screen of his laptop once again. "Your mother worked for the government under the name of Tatiana Lopez. I don't have details on exactly what she did, but I suspect she was an undercover CIA operative. All the files on her are completely locked so I'm unable to get more information, but it did have a symbol by her name which indicated that she is indeed deceased."

"How did you find all that out?" she asked as she listened intently.

"I can't tell you that," Malik said. "Let's just say I know just as many high people in high places as I do low people in low places."

"Okay," she said motioning her hands for him to tell her more. "What about my sister?" Malik's smile slightly faltered.

"Just tell me," she stated firmly. "I can handle it."

"Your sister, Raina Howard, is living in Indianapolis," Malik said as he took another deep breath. "She's married with two children."

"Did she grow up in foster care?" Mya asked.

"Only for a couple years," Malik stated. "Then she was adopted by two doctors."

"Doctors?" Mya said as her voice clogged with emotion. "So I'm guessing she's had a good life."

"It seems that way," Malik said as he leaned to her and enclosed her hands in his. "But no matter how she was raised, she's still your sister. You still have living family."

Malik waited for it to sink in that no matter how good of a life her sister had, finding her was still a blessing. He continued to rub her hands as he watched some of the tension finally leave her face.

"Is she older or younger?" she asked Malik with wide eyes full of curiosity.

Malik got out of his desk chair and motioned for Mya to sit there instead. "I have a picture of her from last school year," Malik said as he began clicking on files over her shoulders. "She's a schoolteacher so like you, she values the importance of education."

His fingers moved across the keys as he located the photo in the files he had on the investigation.

"Are you ready?" he asked glancing down at her.

"I'm ready," she replied as she clenched her hands in her lap. Malik felt just as nervous to show her the picture, as she was anxious to view it.

One. Two. Click.

Chapter 19

Mya's hands flew to her mouth the minute Malik clicked open the photo that contained even more answers to questions about her past. She didn't know what she had expected when Malik opened the image, but she wasn't prepared to have an identical set of almond-shaped brown eyes looking at her with the same type of smile she'd seen reflected in so many of her own pictures. *Same facial structure. Same natural hair flow. Same shoulder shape. Same complexion.*

"Are we—" she said, her voice trailing off in disbelief.

"Identical twins," Malik said finishing the statement for her. "Yes, you are."

Mya lightly touched the screen with her hand. *Raina... My sister Raina.* "I don't even know how to feel right now," she said.

"That's understandable. Finding out you have a sister is one thing, but finding out you have an identical twin sister is a lot for anyone to handle."

Mya couldn't stop staring at the photo. It was mesmerizing to see someone who looked exactly like her who she hadn't met before.

"Did she grow up in Indiana?" she asked when she was finally able to formulate a complete sentence.

"She was placed in an orphanage in Indianapolis, so I assume whomever made your mother give up her children had separated you both purposefully."

Mya was almost afraid to ask him more questions, but she needed to. "Did you find anything on our birth father?"

"No," Malik stated in defeat. "Although you only wanted to find out if you had a sibling, I did a bit of digging around for your birth father after I found some information on your mother. But I came up short."

"That's okay," Mya said touching the screen once more. "Knowing about my mother and sister is fulfillment enough."

Malik reached over her shoulders and handed her a phone.

"Why are you handing me this?" she asked.

"So you can call her," Malik stated. "You want to contact her, right? Maybe even request a DNA test to eliminate any doubt?"

Mya glanced back at the screen. "I'm not sure," she said. "What if she doesn't want to be found?"

"You don't have to worry about that," Malik said. "That's what I was researching this morning when I located the picture. When she turned eighteen she hired an investigator to locate her birth parents and the investigator couldn't find any usable leads. We had the upper hand in our case because of Ms. Bee."

He placed the phone on the desk and began rubbing her shoulders. "She wants to be found, Mya. The search remained active for two years before she gave up. Don't you think you owe it to her to at least contact her?"

Mya knew he was right, but she was so nervous she felt like she could throw up.

"You can do this," he said encouraging her to make the call.

"What if she says she wants to meet me?" Mya asked.

"Then we'll go meet her," Malik responded as he turned the desk chair to face him. He touched both sides of her shoulders. "You're not in this alone," he said in a comforting tone. "Make the call. Here's the number." He pointed to a post-it note she hadn't seen before.

"Okay," she said as she picked up her cell phone with shaky fingers. Mya couldn't believe that after years of wondering if she had any immediate family, she was about to call her twin sister.

She dialed the number and placed the phone on speaker. Sitting there while it rang seemed like the longest seven seconds of her life.

"Hello?" a voice said into the line. *Oh my god, she even sounds like me.*

"Hi," Mya said in a shaky voice. "May I speak to Raina Howard?" she said although Mya knew it was her.

"This is her," Raina said slowly. Mya wondered if

she was picking up on the similarity of their voices as well.

"Raina, my name is Mya Winters," she picked at her fingers nervously. "I know this call is completely out of the blue and I won't blame you if you hang up right now, but I'm—" her voice broke as she tried to finish her statement. "I'm your—" she tried again. Malik motioned for her to take a deep breath.

"My name is Mya Winters and I'm your birth sister," Mya said into the phone. She waited for Raina to deny it or call her a liar. Or even worse, hang up in her face. But Raina didn't say any of that.

"Hello, Mya," Raina said calmly. "I figured out who you must be when you started talking. Call it a sister's intuition."

Mya let out the breath she'd been holding. "I wasn't sure calling you was the right thing to do, so my nerves got the best of me."

"Well I'm really glad you did," Raina said. "I feel like I've waited my entire life to find you."

"I know how you feel," Mya replied. "And we're not just sisters," she said into the phone. She glanced at Malik who gave her a smile of encouragement. "We're actually twins."

"What!" Raina exclaimed into the phone. "We're what! Oh my goodness…" Now it was Mya's turn to be calm while Raina's voice cracked with emotion.

"Mya you have got to stop fidgeting," Malik said as he followed the GPS and turned down the side road.

"I don't fidget," Mya said before dropping her eyes to her hands and realizing she was doing just that.

"I can't help it," she said anxiously. "I'm meeting my sister for the first time. I can't even put into words how this feels."

"You'll be fine, sweetie," Ms. Bee said in the backseat. "I bet it will feel like you and Raina have known each other for years."

When Mya had called Ms. Bee and told her the news about finding her sister, Ms. Bee hadn't been able to stop crying. Even though it had been hard to comprehend the fact that Ms. Bee had kept knowledge of her birth mother a secret for all these years, Mya was really beginning to understand that age-old saying that everything happens for a reason.

Mya and Raina had talked every day for the past week and had immediately made plans to see each other the following weekend. It had been hard telling Raina the story about their mother's recent passing, but finding one another made the news easier for her sister to handle. Through their conversations, Mya had learned that Raina also had two older brothers, six nieces and nephews, and although Raina's parents were divorced, both parents had remarried and were now in happy relationships.

You can do this, she said to herself as she tried to calm her nerves. She'd even been nervous the day before when she'd finally opened up to her friends and Elite Events partners about the investigation. They'd hugged. They'd cried. And in true Elite Events fashion, the ladies were already planning a girls-only weekend to get to know Raina after her and Mya had time to reconnect and get to know one another.

As they turned into the cul-de-sac, Mya's mouth dropped in awe.

"Well I'll be," Ms. Bee said peering out the window. "If this isn't the definition of a warm welcome, I don't know what is."

Malik stopped three cars down from the address they'd entered into the navigational system. Mya glanced around at the thirty-plus people scattered around the cul-de-sac. "I thought she said a few people," Mya stated as she watched the crowd come to the car. *What if they don't like me?* She'd only known Raina for a week, but she could tell they were complete opposites. Even with the differences in personality, they'd still felt like they had known each other forever.

"You'll be fine," Malik said giving her hands a tight squeeze.

"You both know it takes me a while to open up to people," she said staring at all the happy faces. "I can already tell that Raina is way more comfortable talking about certain things than I am." She glanced at Malik. "My past was so different than hers. I don't even know how to begin."

"Just start from the beginning," he said as he brushed his fingers through her hair and brought her closer for a kiss. "No one said you had to divulge your entire life story in one day. Everything takes time." Malik looked outside at the people crowding the car. "But I'd say you're one lucky woman to have so many people ready to meet you and get to know you."

Mya took a deep breath. "Okay, I'm ready," she said as she placed her hand on the handle and opened the door. The first person she noticed was Raina who was standing there with a welcome sign and eyes full of tears. Mya noticed that everyone had stood back to let them have this moment. Her feet felt extremely heavy as she walked closer to Raina. She thought it would be weird to meet a woman who looked exactly like her, but instead, she felt complete. Like all the hardships in her life had prepared her for this exact moment.

As she got closer to Raina, Mya felt her footsteps quicken. She had told herself she wouldn't cry, but the moment was too monumental for her not to shed a tear or two. When they were in arm's reach, Raina pulled Mya into her arms as they cried together.

"I often thought I was crazy with the way I would think something in my head and then answer it," Raina said in her ear. "Now I know that I wasn't crazy, I was talking to you."

Mya hugged Raina even tighter after her statement. "I would often imagine that I had a sister to talk to after years of being alone and having no one to rely on but myself," Mya admitted. "Now I realize what was happening."

"I was there every time," Raina said as she wiped the tears from Mya's eyes. "And now any time you need me, I'm just a phone call away."

The smile Raina wore mirrored the smile that was spread across Mya's face.

"Maybe we should start introductions now," Raina suggested. On cue, Ms. Bee walked over and quickly introduced herself before giving Raina a big hug.

"It's great to meet you, Mrs. Bee," Raina said returning her hug. "Let me introduce you both to my husband, kids and everyone else," Raina said as she locked arms with Mya. "And you have to introduce me to that hunk standing at the car gawking at you," Raina whispered. "Is that Malik?"

Mya glanced over her shoulder at Malik who was leaning on the car smiling at her with those sexy lips that often left her speechless. "Yup," she said as she waved him over to join her. "The one and only."

Chapter 20

Two months later...

"Malik, the wedding starts in five hours, so we need to get some rest."

"I only need three hours to function tomorrow," Malik said as he placed kisses along her spine. "The other two will just go to waste."

"If this is your way of convincing me to turn over so we can have sex, this is a poor argument," Mya said into her pillow.

The entire wedding party and wedding guests were staying in the host hotel for Lex and Micah's fall wedding. At first, the women had all agreed to share a room so they could each get a good night's sleep before tomorrow, but when the men got wind of their plans, that idea went out the window.

"You know I haven't been feeling well," Mya said. "And with the after-school program opening last week, I've gotten zero sleep."

"I know," Malik replied as his lips moved from her spine to her neck. "That's why I'm trying to make you feel better."

Malik really hadn't liked how busy Mya had been lately, but between their trips to Detroit and Indiana to visit Mya's new family, they were both exhausted.

After deciding that they needed to make some serious life decisions, Malik had agreed to make his main home Chicago and keep his office and properties in Detroit. He was glad he'd made the decision, and being in the same city as his brother, cousins, and Mya was well worth it.

"And how exactly is having sex going to make me feel better?"

"Sex makes everything better," he said moving from her neck down to her thighs. He started to nudge her open with his knees.

"Okay, okay," she said as she flipped over onto her back. "Clearly you're not giving up."

"Never," he said with a sly smile as he made his way up her body. Malik couldn't remember a time in his life when he'd been happier than he was now.

He hovered over her and lightly traced the outline of her face. "Who would have thought we would have ended up here," he said.

"I certainly could not have predicted this," Mya said searching his eyes. "But I can't tell you how happy I am that we got here."

"Me too," Malik said as he leaned down and placed his lips over hers. Malik didn't think he could ever grow tired of tasting Mya and by the way she responded to him, he knew that fact remained true to her as well.

His hands roamed over her body, touching and stroking wherever he pleased. When Mya arched her back at the feel of his fingers between her legs, he slipped in between her folds twirling his fingers inside her core.

"Malik," she gasped as he matched the movement of his fingers in her center to imitate the movement of his tongue in her mouth.

"I need you to come for me," he said into her ear as he briefly left her mouth. When she began moaning in between their kisses and her muscles tightened over his fingers, he circled his thumb over her hard nub, working her all at once.

The triple action sent her right over the edge and Malik leaned up in the bed and watched the range of emotions cross her face.

"I'll never get tired of seeing you come," he said as he feathered her face with light kisses.

"I'll never get tired of you making me come," she said with a satisfied smile.

"In case I haven't told you enough," Malik said hovering over her again, "I am so in love with you, Ms. Winters."

She gazed up at him with glassy eyes. "I'm so in love with you too, Malik," she said, cupping his face.

"I admire everything about you," Malik continued. "Your strength astounds me. Your drive and determination are extremely sexy. And your wittiness keeps me on my toes." He ran his fingers up and down her arm before twirling circles in her hand with his finger. "On top of being beautiful and intelligent, what I love about you the most is that you're a survivor and you didn't look at me as damaged goods, but rather saw me for the man that I was and the father that I hope to be one day."

He dropped the item he'd had in his hand into her open palm. Mya's eyes widened as she gripped the object and brought it up to her face.

"Are you proposing?" she said in shock as the diamond glistened when the streak of moonlight hit it at the perfect angle.

"That's exactly what I'm doing, Mya Winters, soon to be Mya Madden."

She looked down at the rock in her hand and glanced back up at him.

"I had no idea," she said as her eyes began filling with tears.

"I hope that's a yes," he said with loving eyes.

She gave him a sly smirk before slipping the ring on her finger and bringing his face to hers for a kiss. "Of course it's a yes," Mya said as she continued to adorn him with kisses. "I really didn't expect you to propose the day before Lex and Micah's wedding."

"I had to," Malik said with a laugh. "There was no way I was letting you attend this wedding without letting every man in the room know that you are mine."

"I'm pretty sure you already made that known at the rehearsal dinner last night," Mya said with a laugh. Malik thought about the way he'd worked Mya's name into his best-man speech.

"I had to let them know," he said with a laugh.

"I think they got the message loud and clear," she replied. She suddenly began searching his eyes.

"What is it?" he asked with concern.

She bit her bottom lip and glanced away from him. "I wasn't going to tell you this tonight," she said as she met his eyes again.

"What is it?" he asked again when she didn't elaborate.

"Well," she said with a slight smile. "Just so you know, I stick by what I said and I still want to offer a home for a child who could benefit from our love."

Malik studied her eyes in confusion. "I don't get it," he said.

Mya took his hand and gently placed it over her stomach. Malik's eyes grew big with amazement. "It can't be," Malik said as he looked down at her stomach as if looking at it would give him the answer he was searching for.

"I took a pregnancy test last week," Mya said. "Just to be sure, I took four different tests from three different brands. I have my second doctor's appointment on Tuesday. I had planned on telling you after the wedding tomorrow."

"How far along are you?" he asked. They'd had a few mishaps with protection and Mya had told him she wasn't on birth control, but never in a million years did he think he would receive this news.

"I'm five weeks," she said as she placed her hand over his. "But our baby is definitely in there."

"But the doctor said the chances were slim."

"That may be the case, but it happened and I couldn't wait any longer to tell you."

Malik dropped his face to her chest as he traced slow circles on her belly. In that moment, words couldn't describe the range of emotions transpiring through his body. He agreed with Mya, he still wanted to adopt. But he also acknowledged that her getting pregnant was truly a blessing. One that he hadn't ever expected.

"I just can't believe it," Malik said as his voice caught in his throat.

"I know, baby," Mya said as she placed a kiss on his forehead. "Believe me, I know."

Standing at the edge of the dance floor, Mya looked around the room at all the guests enjoying the second Elite Events wedding of the year. As usual, her eyes caught Malik's who rewarded her with a wink and that sexy side smile he'd been sporting all morning. He was wearing his classic black glasses again...the ones that she loved so much. She'd thought about telling him just how much when she saw him putting them on in the morning, but decided to wait. It felt good having at least one secret that he hadn't picked up on yet.

Her eyes searched the dance floor for her friends and partners, as she thought about how much things had changed for them in the past few years. Earlier in the year, she'd watched her friends with envy as she'd questioned if she would ever experience true happiness like the kind that had been reflected in their eyes. Now, thinking back to the past six months, she couldn't believe how much her life had changed for the better.

"Looking for us?" Imani said sneaking up from behind her in a coral bridesmaid's dress that matched the one Mya wore.

"Actually, I was," Mya said with a smile. Last night, Malik and Mya had decided to wait until after Lex and Micah's wedding to announce that they were expecting. But for some reason, she didn't think she could hold the news until then.

"Are you okay?" Lex asked as she rubbed her shoulder. Lex looked stunning in her floor-length all-lace wedding gown and Micah hadn't been able to take his eyes off her all night.

"You're not having second thoughts about marrying Malik, are you?" Cyd asked.

"I'm fine," Mya said as she gently swiped a tear. "And I'm definitely not having second thoughts about Malik. He's everything I never thought I'd find."

"I never thought I'd hear the day when Mya Winters would say those words about a man," Imani said with a smirk. "I'm glad you finally came to your senses."

"We all are," Lex added.

"Thanks, ladies," she said as she stole a glance at Malik who was standing with her friends' significant others.

"If it isn't the engagement, what has you so emotional?" Cyd asked with concern.

Mya glanced at each of the women, unsure if she should keep her secret or not.

"You might as well just spit it out," Imani said as she crossed her arms over her chest followed by similar sentiments from Cyd and Lex.

Mya glanced over at Malik and silently pleaded with him to let her tell her friends. After he shook his head at her and laughed, he finally mouthed *okay*.

"What's with the eye talk?" Cyd asked when she looked back to the group.

"Malik and I were going to wait to tell you all until after Lex and Micah's wedding, but...we're having a baby," Mya blurted out suddenly, too excited to hold it in any longer.

All three women rushed to her at once and bombarded her with a much-needed hug. They never forced Mya to talk about her past, but they'd always known they were the family she never had. Even though she'd found her sister, nothing could ever replace the women who were embracing her now.

"No wonder you're so emotional," Imani said with a smile.

"Oh, Mya, that's amazing news," Lex exclaimed.

"You're going to make a great mom," Cyd added.

While Mya was explaining the details of the proposal and how Malik found out she was pregnant, the men approached, obviously unable to stay away from their wives and future wife any longer.

"I think telling them was the right thing to do," Malik said as he placed a soft kiss on her lips.

"You told the guys?" she asked with a laugh.

"I know I only just found out last night, but I'm excited about our future son," he said with a sly grin.

"You mean, our future daughter," she replied with a knowing look.

Malik nuzzled her neck before bringing his lips to her ear. "How about we don't have this debate until the doctor can reveal the sex of our baby," he suggested.

"That works," Mya said as she wrapped her arms around his neck. "We'll wait until the doctor officially tells us it's a girl."

* * * * *

One legendary clan

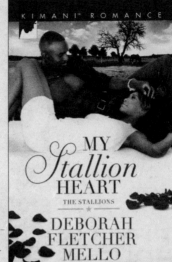

MY *Stallion* HEART

DEBORAH FLETCHER MELLO

Supermodel Natalie Stallion is called back to her hometown from London to settle her mother's estate. But when a nor'easter delays her plans and strands her with Tinjin Braddy, they take full advantage of the delay. The continent-hopping playboy doesn't expect to see her again. But their lives and careers are about to collide at a Stallion family reunion…

THE STALLIONS

★

"Drama, hot sex, attention to detail and a thrilling storyline filled with twists and turns make this book a hard one to put down. A must read."
—*RT Book Reviews* on *HEARTS AFIRE*

Available May 2015!

HARLEQUIN®
™ www.Harlequin.com

KPDFM4010515

Desire is more than skin-deep

Moonlight *Kisses*

PHYLLIS BOURNE

It's just Sage Matthews's luck that Cole Sinclair, the man stirring her dormant passions, wants to buy her cosmetics company. Takeover bid: denied. But in the bedroom, their rivalry morphs into sizzling chemistry. The kind of partnership Sage craves takes compromise and trust—do they have the courage to go beyond the surface to find what's real?

"A memorable tale of letting go of the past and taking risks. The characters are strong, relatable and will inspire readers to carve their own place in history." —*RT Book Reviews* on *SWEETER TEMPTATION*

www.Harlequin.com

Available May 2015!

KPPB4040515

Harmony Evans

Winning Her Love

Bay Point mayor Gregory Langston wants community activist Vanessa Hamilton to help run his reelection campaign. Their attraction is a potential powder keg, especially when they are on opposite sides of a controversial issue. But a vicious smear campaign could destroy Gregory's shot at a second term. Will it also cost him forever with Vanessa?

Bay Point Confessions

"With endearing and believable characters whose struggles mirror real-life family dramas, the unique storyline captures the reader's attention from start to finish."
—*RT Book Reviews* on *STEALING KISSES*

HARLEQUIN®
www.Harlequin.com

Available May 2015!

KPHE4020515

REQUEST YOUR FREE BOOKS!

2 FREE NOVELS PLUS 2 FREE GIFTS!

KIMANI™ ROMANCE

Love's ultimate destination!

YES! Please send me 2 FREE Harlequin® Kimani™ Romance novels and my 2 FREE gifts (gifts are worth about $10). After receiving them, if I don't wish to receive any more books, I can return the shipping statement marked "cancel." If I don't cancel, I will receive 4 brand-new novels every month and be billed just $5.44 per book in the U.S. or $5.99 per book in Canada. That's a savings of at least 16% off the cover price. It's quite a bargain! Shipping and handling is just 50¢ per book in the U.S. and 75¢ per book in Canada.* I understand that accepting the 2 free books and gifts places me under no obligation to buy anything. I can always return a shipment and cancel at any time. Even if I never buy another book, the two free books and gifts are mine to keep forever.

168/368 XDN GH4P

Name _____ (PLEASE PRINT) _____

Address _____ Apt. # _____

City _____ State/Prov. _____ Zip/Postal Code _____

Signature (if under 18, a parent or guardian must sign)

Mail to the **Reader Service:**

IN U.S.A.: P.O. Box 1867, Buffalo, NY 14240-1867
IN CANADA: P.O. Box 609, Fort Erie, Ontario L2A 5X3

Want to try two free books from another line?
Call 1-800-873-8635 or visit www.ReaderService.com.

* Terms and prices subject to change without notice. Prices do not include applicable taxes. Sales tax applicable in N.Y. Canadian residents will be charged applicable taxes. Offer not valid in Quebec. This offer is limited to one order per household. Not valid for current subscribers to Harlequin® Kimani™ Romance books. All orders subject to credit approval. Credit or debit balances in a customer's account(s) may be offset by any other outstanding balance owed by or to the customer. Please allow 4 to 6 weeks for delivery. Offer available while quantities last.

Your Privacy—The Reader Service is committed to protecting your privacy. Our Privacy Policy is available online at www.ReaderService.com or upon request from the Reader Service.

We make a portion of our mailing list available to reputable third parties that offer products we believe may interest you. If you prefer that we not exchange your name with third parties, or if you wish to clarify or modify your communication preferences, please visit us at www.ReaderService.com/consumerchoice or write to us at Reader Service Preference Service, P.O. Box 9062, Buffalo, NY 14240-9062. Include your complete name and address.

KROM15

The first two
stories in the
Love in the Limelight
series, where four
unstoppable women
find fame, fortune
and ultimately…
true love.

LOVE IN THE
LIMELIGHT

New York Times
bestselling author
**BRENDA
JACKSON**
&
A.C. ARTHUR

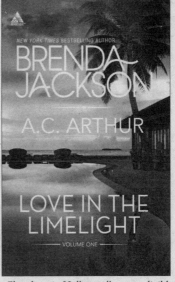

In *Star of His Heart*, Ethan Chambers is Hollywood's most eligible
bachelor. But when he meets his costar Rachel Wellesley, he suddenly
finds himself thinking twice about staying single.

In *Sing Your Pleasure*, Charlene Quinn has just landed a major
contract with L.A.'s hottest record label, working with none other than
Akil Hutton. Despite his gruff attitude, she finds herself powerfully
attracted to the driven music producer.

Available now wherever books are sold!

HARLEQUIN®
www.Harlequin.com

KPLIM11631014R

The last two stories in the *Love in the Limelight* series, where four unstoppable women find fame, fortune and ultimately…true love

LOVE IN THE LIMELIGHT
— VOLUME TWO —

ANN CHRISTOPHER
&
ADRIANNE BYRD

In *Seduced on the Red Carpet*, supermodel Livia Blake is living a glamorous life…but when she meets sexy single father Hunter Chambers, she is tempted with desire and a life that she has never known.

In *Lovers Premiere*, Sofia Wellesley must cope as Limelight Entertainment prepares to merge with their biggest rival. Which means dealing with her worst enemy, Ram Jordan. So why is her traitorous heart clamoring for the man she hates most in the world?

Available now!

HARLEQUIN®
www.Harlequin.com

KPLIM21641114R

It may be the biggest challenge she's ever faced...

NAUGHTY

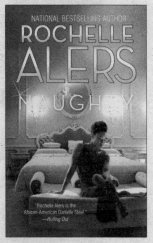

National Bestselling Author

ROCHELLE ALERS

Parties, paparazzi, red-carpet catfights and shocking sex tapes—wild child Breanna Parker has always used her antics to gain attention from her R & B–diva mother and record-producer father. But now, as her whirlwind marriage to a struggling actor implodes, Bree is ready to live life on her own terms, and the results will take everyone—including Bree—by surprise.

"Rochelle Alers is the African-American Danielle Steel."
—*Rolling Out*

"This one's a page-turner with a very satisfying conclusion."
—*RT Book Reviews* on *SECRET VOWS*

Available now!

www.Harlequin.com

KPRA1690115R

Two classic novels featuring the sexy and sensational Westmoreland family…

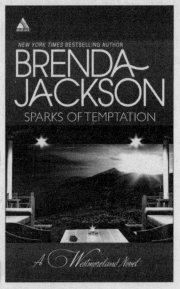

SPARKS OF TEMPTATION

New York Times Bestselling Author

BRENDA JACKSON

The moment Jason Westmoreland meets Bella Bostwick in *The Proposal*, he wants her—and the land she's inherited. With one convenient proposal, he could have the Southern beauty in his bed and her birthright in his hands. But that's only if Bella says yes…

The affair between Dr. Micah Westmoreland and Kalina Daniels ended too abruptly. Now that they are working side by side, he can't ignore the heat that still burns between them. And he plans to make her his… in *Feeling the Heat*.

"Jackson's love scenes are hot and steamy and her storyline believable enough to make readers beg for more."
—RT Book Reviews on *PRIVATE ARRANGEMENTS*

Available now!

HARLEQUIN®
www.Harlequin.com

KPBJI700215R